All That Road GOING

All That

A.G. MOJTABAI

Road GOING

A Novel

TRIQUARTERLY BOOKS
NORTHWESTERN UNIVERSITY PRESS
EVANSTON, ILLINOIS

Northwestern University Press
www.nupress.northwestern.edu

Printed in the United States of America

10 9 8 7 6 5 4 3 2 1

This is a work of fiction. Characters, places, and events are the product of the
author's imagination or are used fictitiously and do not represent actual people,
places, or events.

Library of Congress Cataloging-in-Publication Data

Mojtabai, A. G., 1937–
    All that road going : a novel / A.G. Mojtabai.
    p. cm.
    ISBN-13: 978-0-8101-5200-7 (trade cloth : alk. paper)
    ISBN-10: 0-8101-5200-2 (trade cloth : alk. paper)
    1. Bus travel—United States—Fiction. I. Title.
    PS3563.O374A58 2008
    813.54—dc22
                                                2007050454

∞ The paper used in this publication meets the minimum requirements of the
American National Standard for Information Sciences—Permanence of Paper for
Printed Library Materials, ANSI Z39.48-1992.

For
Joaquín, Shahrzad, and Cyrus

So in America when the sun goes down and I sit on the old broken-down river pier watching the long, long skies over New Jersey and sense all that raw land that rolls in one unbelievable huge bulge over to the West Coast, and all that road going, all the people dreaming in the immensity of it . . .

Jack Kerouac, *On the Road*

It's over. The world wakes up.

The wasted passion stuns, as a cloud
Might pass across the mind's eye,
The dream of life opaque to life.

Alfred Corn, "April"

All That Road GOING

One

Door

HIS COMPANION WAS A SMOKER WITH A CRACKLING LAUGH sounding not much different from his cough. Add a beat—it was the same. Pierson found himself shrinking into his own corner; the man's legs, splayed out in a gaping V, crowded him. Not that Pierson took up all that much space—he'd always been slight, built like a sprinter, they used to say—but he'd paid in full, he was entitled to a full seat.

Damn right—entitled!

The man told Pierson he was a trucker deadheading from Bakersfield, California, to Joplin, Missouri. Joplin's where he set out from three days ago. Had a house in Carthage. Semidetached, but he was only a renter. "Rent goes nowhere," he was wise on that. Problem was, he still couldn't afford a mortgage on anything. "No way to live!" he said, shaking his head as if Pierson had said something to contradict him, then sighed and started in on his health. His nerves were shot, his chest rattled, even lying down. Got so bad he saw sparks when he coughed. He'd been used to driving fifteen hours at a stretch, thought nothing of it, except for his aching back. And he'd be willing to put up with all those aches and pains, all the frustrations—the chuck holes, the oil slicks, construction detours and weigh stations, the wind and the weather, the lonely nights—if only he could count on the extra cash. He was paid by the mile, but now they'd cut back on hours allowed behind the wheel and he couldn't pack in the miles, there was no extra cash. "The ICC's got all these rules and regulations tying us up in knots. Government out to get you any which way you look."

Only time he felt top of the heap was roaring down the highway, pushing the limit. Fancy rig, a Kenworth or one of those Peterbilts, chrome stacks chugging away. Riding high in his cab, tall enough to spit on everybody else, watching the hatchbacks and compacts—piss ants, all—scoot left and right to make way for him.

"Pipes, lumber, mufflers, mushrooms to Laredo . . ." He'd hauled just about everything in his time, to hear tell. "No live cattle—but tons of swinging beef. Hauled a mess of toxic hogs over the border, down to old Me-hi-co. Suppose to be burned up. I sure hope they did." Hadn't waited around to make sure.

What he liked best was zipping through Wyoming and Montana, making time, whatever speed he could handle. Summer driving, early fall, late spring—the rest of the year was hell. "You know what they say about Wyoming?"

Pierson didn't know, didn't need to—the punch line was already launched.

"That's a state where the men are men, the women are jealous, and the sheep are nervous." He paused then, waiting through Pierson's silence for any kind of ripple—none forthcoming. Finally, he said, "You probably heard that one before?"

Pierson hadn't but nodded anyway; it seemed the shortest way.

It made no difference, say or don't say; the voice beside him kept on, never resting. No participation required. Pierson tried staring out the window but found nothing to latch his eye onto.

Idling fields (seen one, you've seen 'em all), telephone poles ticking past, threading mile to mile, a battered billboard, advertising SINCERE SERVICE—for what? Not a clue: the rest of the message was weathered down to bare boards.

Years back, the man said, he'd just about lived in his truck. Got in the habit of calling it his, even though he never owned it. But he'd stuck with the same company and they stuck by him, and the work was steady so he did manage to put some money by. Did most of his cooking by popping the hood and setting a can of franks and beans on the carburetor. "That was in the old days— the old trucks," which nobody wanted to go back to, but—"you can't win." He sighed again.

Pierson tried to back off in his mind, tried to picture how a stranger might see the two of them: the trucker, fortyish, in unwashed jeans and a T-shirt advertising (a joke, surely) a town called Muleshoe, Texas. Then Pierson himself (pushing seventy, though he flattered himself that he could still pass for fifty-some) in a cream-colored jacket and pale-blue shirt with fine white stripes. The jacket looked like pure linen, though linen was only a percentage of the blend; it was mostly polyester to withstand crushing. Pierson knew how to shop for things, he didn't need a woman for that.

"What line of work you say you're in?" the trucker asked.

Pierson hadn't said but had no choice this time. "Sales— retired," he obliged, wasting not a syllable.

Pierson's leg was acting up again, his old charley horse, it would soon be all he could think of. Stiffening and flexing his right foot, he tried to quiet the quaking of his calf—useless—then brought his left leg down over his right, tamping it down by main force. He blinked, hard, till water sprang from the corners of his eyes. Strain as he might, his lids couldn't seem to stay pried apart, his head kept swinging, his mind winking off. He wasn't sleeping, quite, wasn't fully awake, only half dreaming. *How'd they say it— "mind's eye?"* Dipping and catching himself, he was whipsawed into seeing. Sharp as anything: the room, the bed, Marie's lips beaded with bubbles, voice burbling, "Wait . . . wait . . . wait." She was drowned but didn't know it. His gaze kept circling round and round her: door, bed, window, door, bed, doorknob, hand—his hand, the apple of the knob solid in his hand, the hallway gleaming . . .

"Did I say something?" the trucker turned to Pierson, his brow creased with concern.

"No, why?" Pierson's eyes blinked open.

"Your face," he said. "The look on your face."

WHEN THE NURSE LED HIM OUT OF MARIE'S ROOM TO "HAVE a word" with him in the corridor, and the word turned out to be, "Your wife could die tonight," it didn't do a thing to change Pierson's mind. First off, Marie wasn't his wife; they'd been living together was all. Living together for how long? Twenty-some years, so happened, but since when did arithmetic have anything to do with anything?

. . . But suppose the nurse had said, "She's dying"—instead of "could die tonight," suppose she'd said "is" instead of "could," allowing no maybes, no wiggle room—would he do anything any different? Suppose the doctor had said, "You're trying to outrun death—it can't be done . . ."

He'd still run.

Didn't matter how they said it: Pierson could see for himself what was what. He didn't need a tour to tell him what business hospice was in. But why hadn't he seen it coming?

He wasn't ready.

She was foaming when they wheeled her over the bridge from the hospital, hair foaming round her face, words sudsing from her lips—half of them lost, all meaning lost, bottled up in the mask—crazed by the drugs they were giving her and whatever she was going through. Maybe it was the panic of the mask making her wild, they wondered, and they tried switching to another device, something more open. Two little straws up her nose, all it amounted to, but Marie kept pulling the straws out,

All That Road GOING

kept touching the tips to the far corners of her eyes. So, panicked or not, there'd been no help for it—it had to be the full mask.

Pierson could recognize scraps of her usual worries coming through: bills unpaid, coupons she'd squirreled away, her keys, her wallet . . . Had he remembered to bring her handbag? He had. He was carrying it even as she asked, couldn't she see for herself? He lifted it, waved it inches from her face. Carrying a woman's handbag, for cripes sake! *Must of looked like a fool . . .*

Add to that, he could swear she was singing. Something about travel. It was no song he'd ever heard. It was crazy—Marie's travels were done. This would be her last room, her final bed. A crucifix hung over the bed, a girlish figure draped upon it. Could have been sunbathing on the beach with legs so coyly dangled. Basking in pain, asking for it . . . Pierson felt his anger building. Marie's voice burbled on. Made him feel near breathless himself, trapped in a singing, choking mist.

Then, his back to the bed, staring at the folded towels and bed liners stacked in readiness, as he bent to stow Marie's handbag in the cabinet under the sink, this strange thing happened. He watched his hand move like a glove or somebody else's hand, two fingers, one long, one short, springing the clasp, then the other brothers trailing after them into the depths of the bag. Five fingers capering on their own, browsing for whatever, whatever they might happen to find. Lipstick, cough drops, crumpled tissues . . . pillbox, compact, change purse, keys, and wallet . . . How silken smooth the leather sliding from fingers to palm. For safekeeping, he told himself, pocketing the wallet—leaving the keys behind. And, standing in the Greyhound terminal, under the double sign suspended from the ceiling—white on blue, blue on white—that said on one face ¿DÓNDE QUIERES IR? and on the other WHERE DO YOU WANT TO GO? Pierson told himself he couldn't have known beforehand that, within the hour, he'd be slapping the wallet onto the ticket counter and emptying the thing, all but two dollars, to pay for a See America pass and a trip clear across the country. How could he have known? Marie was raving was all he knew, as he—Pierson—soon would be if he stuck around much longer.

The intake rigmarole had been endless, a shitload of paperwork, most of it fussing about how the medical bills would be paid. He stood by her for as long as it lasted, though; he'd signed and dated, signed and dated, *yes, yes, yes,* wherever the *X* told him to sign. He'd been nailed, over and over—wasn't that enough?

Add to driving him crazy the nurse being called away every two minutes, with Marie's talking-singing rant picking up soon as the nurse stepped out. Leaving Pierson alone to pace Marie's bedside. He'd near the door, then veer back in an ever-widening circle, the golden, gleaming doorknob the apple of his eye. He had no plan— only that image, that golden gleam. But Marie, quick as ever, was on to him: she'd start calling out his name when he got anywhere near the door. Then—other names he didn't catch. One minute, she'd be lying in her hospice bed, sick as a dog, unable to lift a foot, next—she was off to a barn dance, do-si-do, round and round, dancing with somebody called Ray, playing rummy with somebody called Cody . . .

Raving!

Pilot, Here

WE'D BEEN HAVING ONE OF THOSE CLOVER DAYS IN EARLY April, golden, glossy, everything buttered with sunshine, buds fattening, bird sounds—bright sounds—I won't say "songs," not all birds sing.

Been a lot of rain in the area. You could smell it yet: deep earth mint and dung, the air drenched with it. "A million-dollar rain," wheat farmers called it, giving guarded thanks. Another frost was still possible, though unlikely—fifteenth of the month was pretty much the deadline on that. The depot was bustling, more passengers milling around than I'd seen in months—Christmas and New Year's excepted. People cooped up all winter long, itching to be up, out, and moving on. Personally, I've never shared that itch. Couldn't think of anything better than staying home, staying put. Just my personal opinion.

I was thinking of my lawn, only now starting to repay long hours of tending. I'd planted fescue and the green was crowding up, overtaking the old straws of Bermuda. Already my pear trees were going from bloom to leaf. Might even have a little fruit this year, but I wasn't counting on it. All I really wanted was to feast my eyes on that new green—looking forward to my three days off next week, a chance to weed a little, and then just to set on the porch enjoying the view, not lifting a finger, watching my teenagers take on the mowing. That's a sight I really do relish!

Should have known some clouds would be waiting in the wings. By the time my bus came in, we were already twenty minutes behind schedule. Top of that, it was a great piece of junk they'd handed me: 8213. I recognized the old girl right off the bat—I'd driven this beauty before.

She'd been around: had a permanent sway to the right, a kink in the steering wheel, and an off-again, on-again heating system. I reminded the dispatcher of these facts. He shrugged, promising better luck next time. The bus that should have been mine was running second section on the Albuquerque to L.A. schedule; there'd been an overflow crowd for that particular run. Nothing I could do but sound off, then forget it. I could only count on about an hour of daylight—hour and a half at best—before full dark. The dispatcher wished me "Happy trails!" and left me to it.

So I went about my business, double-checking the control panel: oil gauge, gas, turn signals, wipers, lights, adjusting the side views, the rearview passenger mirror, then stepping out to bump the tires and oversee the baggage loading in progress— really, to josh a minute with Mike and Ray, the guys handling it. And finally, to have a glance at the new boarders lining up at gate 3. My eye made a quick tally: sixteen, there'd be enough—barely enough—seats for everyone this leg of the road but no guarantees after that. Unless most of these were short run—which would ease things. I'd have to warn them about not spreading out all over the place.

I slid my name card into the holder. That's the regulation, standard operating procedure, not worth mentioning but for the fact that letting people know your name is one of those details a bunch of drivers I know prefer to forget nowadays. I understand their way of thinking: time like ours, you never know who's going to be suing you for what. It's a real concern. But I—call it foolish if you like—still think that meeting people name to name, face to face, is what it's all about.

So, anyway, I gave them my name: O. M. Plumlee. *O* stands for Orville. Kind of old-fashioned—my mother was thinking of the Wright brothers at the time. *M* is the letter I go by: for Matt, short for Matthew. But, speaking professionally, I don't think a little formality is a bad thing. Any complaints? O. M. Plumlee's the name. Got a word of praise? Same name. O. M. Plumlee— pilot, here.

My habit is to size up my passengers right away. Going by the tally handed me, there were twenty-nine continuing on from points west. Those few traveling all the way, coast to coast, met my stare with glazed eyes. By now they'd seen a number of drivers come and go. Starting my shift in Oklahoma City, I was one of the middle ones in the lineup—but, at this point, I guess we all looked the same to them.

Some of the passengers stood out from the first. Like this black couple up near the front—pleasing smiles, well spoken. Extra friendly, could *not* be nicer—toting a baby too young to travel. The baby was starting to squirm, only letting off a little steam as yet, but I expected we'd be hearing from her—and plenty—in the future.

One young lady used the opportunity to press me on when exactly we'd be arriving in St. Louis. I had to admit we were running a bit behind schedule but I'd do my best to make up the time. Good-looking gal: curly headed, ringlets all over, with long black lashes, gold hoops in her ears, so I added, "Just for you," and smiled.

"It's real important," she said. She was too young to look serious without frowning. "It's my first wedding anniversary. Tomorrow is one week to the day!" I offered my congratulations.

"We're Roberta and Robert Wright," she wanted me to know, "R and R, for short."

"Sounds like you're custom cut for each other," I said. I made some mention of her ticket being a reissue, not the original. *Big* mistake, as it turned out, enough to get her started, spilling out all her business: how they'd had their first big blowup and she'd split, bought herself a one-way to California, but only made it as far as Tucson, where she'd been paged by you'd-never-guess-who.

"Must've wanted you back," I handed the ticket over.

"I know it. He'll be waiting for me in St. Louis . . ."

And she would have gone on. But this was getting to be somewhat of a social event, and I had work to do. "Can't promise you on the time," I said. "Best I can do is try."

The problem passenger—*one* of the problems—I could spot right off the bat. Way in the back, where he'd spread out to occupy the entire double seat—small duffle on the window side, and a metal lunch box clamped to his lap. The one who seemed to be humming to himself, and who tried to make me think he was deaf when I reminded him that he couldn't count on a double seat after the next stop, and then shot his deaf act to smithereens by blasting back with, "It's a free country!"—proving that he'd heard me all right the first time. No fun with this one! This one was pure meanness, trouble waiting to happen—or maybe already had. Looking over his ticket, I did wonder about his turnaround in Pittsburgh. Why travel halfway across the country only to about-face and come right back? Only bus drivers and truckers did that.

I pride myself on being a reader of human nature, but, with this fellow, I couldn't even begin. He wasn't one of those aging hippies I saw all too many of—a hippie would've punched out those frayed knees and elbows, worn them with pride—while *his* frayed spots were carefully mended. This one was poor, piss poor, he wasn't putting on an act. And the winter wool cap he was wearing, one of those navy watch caps, pulled down to his eyebrows—what was the story there? Cold? Balding? In hiding? Or his own peculiar idea of style?

He had me puzzling from the start . . . like his hailing from some little way station in Montana. Out in the boonies, my guess.

Platow—the name was on the coupon; I reminded myself to try and find it on the map at our first rest stop. *If* I managed to keep it in mind till then . . . The ticket—a fat little book of coupons, the kind you hardly ever see anymore, written out by hand in carbon triplicates—told me he was coming from a place untouched by computers, well out of the mainstream. But the man himself didn't strike me as a country type, at least—not country born and bred.

Another thing: I didn't really catch a good whiff of him until I bent over to return his ticket. Then the hot animal smell came back at me: monkey, maybe, or strong fox. Good thing he'd settled himself well to the rear as he had.

A puzzle, like I said, but there wasn't a blessed thing I could put a finger to. Just a feeling: *man with a mental history here.* I didn't know a thing, but was willing to bet on it.

We're leaky creatures, by and large; it's the exception nowadays to find anybody holding back, so it's not the easy talkers, the Robertas of this world, who stand out for me but the ones who aren't saying. This fellow in the knit cap was definitely top of my list. *My list for this trip, so far, but I'm only starting,* I had to remind myself.

Across the aisle from him sat one of those fast-looking gals. Kind that also headed straight for the back of the bus. Could have been a uniform she was wearing: the punk hairdo standing up in spikes, hip-hugger jeans, and skimpy, sleeveless top with bare midriff down to her belly button. Tattoo on one shoulder, a botch job—twisted together serpents or ivy, hard to tell which. No mystery in either case. She'd originated in Barstow and was headed I forget where in Missouri. I'd have given a bunch of bills to know what *she* thought about him—our man from Platow.

BEHIND HIS CLOSED LIDS, PIERSON'S EYES WERE BRIMMING. It was Marie he saw, tucked up in bed. She was swatting flies, swiping at them with both hands, then using her forefinger and thumb, trying to pinch this particular one and that particular one.

Flies all over the sheet—her hands were busy telling him. But, of course, there wasn't a speck on the sheet.

Then her hands got busy with something else. It took a moment to grasp what it was she thought she was doing. The nurse caught on first: "She's working, right? . . . Looks like she's sewing . . ." She turned to Marie: "Are you sewing, Marie? Were you a seamstress?" Marie shook her head, no. "Whai . . . ," she corrected, "rheh . . . sss," her lips shaped the syllables with almost no sound coming out. The mask was transparent, so sometimes you could lip-read, but whatever words came next were lost, blurred in froth.

The nurse shot Pierson a look, as if to ask: *So why is she so busy stitching, then? Is this crazy, or what?* Because she sure did seem to be sewing, sizing the invisible thread and snipping it, her tongue wetting the inside of the mask at the very spot where her hand with the invisible needle touched the plastic from the outside. Then—she should've been an actress!—guiding the invisible thread to meet the invisible needle. And then came the really cunning part, missing the needle's eye twice (the needle that wasn't there, the thread that wasn't there) until it caught on the third try. Then looping it double and making a knot. And, finally, lifting a corner of the sheet that covered her and starting to sew, calming as her fingers slid under and over, in and out. Pierson knew she was stitching him back to her, trying to.

When the nurse entered with medications, Pierson was already on his feet. "Give me a call," he mumbled over his shoulder and scrammed without waiting for reply. *Step on it!* Giant step, dwarf step, jagged to start, right leg shrinking, spurting, stroking along . . .

He shoved open the outer door. Halted, backing up into the dim vestibule, heart still racing. Shocked by the searing light— he'd forgotten it was broad day.

Wait . . . Wait . . .

Anybody? No. Nobody. He was safe. But that light—it was pitiless! Had to brace himself before cracking the door open again.

This time he plunged. *Gotta go—got to!* Already the soles of his feet were sweating. The door cuffed him as it swung, nudging him on his way. He was free—*alive!*—in the glittering air. Then he heard the door suck shut behind him. Then a click.

It was done.

This Girl

OUGHT TO BE OVER IT BY THIS TIME; AFTER ALL, I'VE BEEN driving buses for more than twenty years. But some things never change. Setting out, my feelings are always the same, always double. First off, I never know who I'm going to meet or what might come up. Second—my second thought: I've seen it all, pretty much everything, by now. Things you wouldn't *believe* . . . I've seen quickie marriages consummated in the back of the bus. Well . . . not marriages, quite, and not *seen*, exactly—but glimpsed enough to know what was going on. Don't ask me what happened a few hundred miles down the freeway. Could guess, but it's a rare sight for the same passengers to come round again on my particular shift.

But then, while I was thinking this, the rare thing happened. I recognized this girl, inching forward, in the lineup of new boarders. Already she had her ticket out of the envelope, though it would be a couple of minutes yet until I got round to her. It sure *looked* like the same girl, barely into her teens, snub nosed and freckled with straw-colored hair and, now as before, much too pale for anyone healthy enough to be standing or walking on her own two feet . . . Where was it then? Missouri, someplace. One of those little lost "misery towns" as a smart aleck on board liked to call them. The town was only a flag stop; no real depot, just a doughnut shop doubling as a ticket office, with no direct service anywhere. I could see it clear as yesterday. Hinton? Hanton? Hun— Something. *H*-something Junction . . . Pain in the neck for me: the town of whatever (the name on the tip of my tongue). Some problem with their local connecting bus to the regular depot in Stanton and I'd been called to fill the gap.

Then it came to me. The name was Hunters Junction. A day unseasonably warm. Like Indian summer, in late October . . . I remember thinking that a girl her age ought to be in school. Instead, she was about to set off on a long-distance bus. Alone—I knew right away that she'd be traveling alone, even though she was well fenced in with company at that moment. Church ladies, judging from their hair buns and dark, drab, homemade dresses, cut from the same swatch of cloth, the same pattern—all severe, but for the curious flare of their puff sleeves. They weren't old, those ladies, but so prim and grim it was hard to imagine they'd ever been young. I figured they belonged to one of those hellfire and brimstone holiness churches you're apt to find in backwater towns. We'd passed a billboard coming into town: PLEASE DON'T GO TO HELL. LOVE, JESUS, and it should have been fair warning— the splashes of red and yellow in the background, with this blot, twisted black, in the middle of it, a shape once human maybe but charred beyond recognition. *Whew, boy!* I'd never forget *that*— and how those good ladies had circled the girl and were laying hands on her as I nosed in to park. It was a regular love fest they had going there, and anyone could see how bowed down the girl was, shrinking from all those blessings. My heart went out to her: there's no defense against an attack like that.

Funny . . . Seeing the girl again this time round, how much came back to me, how much I must've stored away. Little things. How red her eyes, for one. Had been crying for quite some time, I expect, then turned to stare off to the side at a boy perched on the curb, biting into a sandwich. Nothing out of the ordinary there, yet I knew exactly what seized her attention. A squirrel had crept close to the boy; he was standing on his hind legs, tail raised up, shape of a question mark, and he was wringing his tiny hands, *asking*. The boy was chewing and spitting, spraying crumbs in the critter's face, trying to blow him away. The girl stared, wide eyed, astonished, at the two of them; my eyes met hers—by a sort of triangulation, you might say.

I'd motioned the girl forward then and unfolded her ticket. Her destination was someplace in Oklahoma I'd never heard of. She'd have to transfer to a local bus or, could be, a couple of buses. I told her this, but it seemed to come as no surprise. So I picked up her suitcase, startled at how light it was (a girl her age), tossing it into the freight compartment, and, touching her elbow to guide her, ushered her on board.

Once inside, she seemed unaware of the tears still streaking her cheeks and made no effort to wipe them away. I guessed her age as fourteen—fifteen tops. She might have been pretty but for her color. Pale as a jailbird. Like she hadn't seen the light of day in years. That wouldn't be natural for someone so young. Could've been sick for a long time, of course . . . I had a hunch that wasn't it.

I even recalled the dress she wore: a long but skimpy cotton thing, dark blue, speckled with white spots fine as salt. She kept plucking the cloth away from her skin. Maybe it was the heat, or some nervous habit she'd always had, but, again, I didn't think so. Like I said, I pretty well guessed what the story was. And that it would have no good ending.

We'd made the briefest of stops for this girl. No one offered to come on board to help her settle in, but that made it all the easier for me—we'd been behind, even before the unexpected detour, and I was glad to be able to take off without further delay. The boy was still squatting curbside as we pulled out, still chewing. Only the crust of his sandwich remained. The squirrel, back

All That Road GOING

down on all fours, had moved a short distance off; he continued to track the boy's movements: something, some small morsel, might yet be tossed his way.

The seat she found was three or four rows back; she settled in, pressing her palm to the window, her face mostly masked off by her hand. Her escorts had located her window by that time, and one of the ladies was tapping on the pane, but the girl sat frozen, motionless, fingers rayed out, pressed flat against the glass, blotting out as much of the scene, and herself, as she could. The ladies must have taken her raised hand for a wave; they all waved back.

I had the air-conditioning going full blast, as I recall, trying to keep myself awake and the passengers off my back. I angled my inside mirror so as to keep my eye on the girl. That moon-pale skin . . . I was a little spooked by how ghostly—afraid she might faint on me. Then, when I noticed her shivering and hunching down, I took the hint and scaled back a notch on the cooling. I could see that her cheeks were still glistening. They dried slowly as the miles wore on. From here on out, no one would know who she was: she was quite safe with us, but she'd wrapped herself in her own arms, in thick silence, and she flinched, actually flinched, when the woman across the aisle ("Alice from Dallas," I'd tagged her), a young gal not that much older than she was, spoke a few harmless words of greeting. The girl said something back—three or four words by way of reply—then returned to her silence, keeping it well wrapped round.

That was then . . . October . . . five months back. So far, I cautioned myself, I'd only spotted this remarkable look-alike in the line of new passengers waiting to board; I couldn't be absolutely sure it was the same girl until I checked her ticket—to see if it said Hunters Junction.

And, at the moment, I had other things on my mind. Everything had been running along pretty smoothly. I'd started the first of the passengers boarding when suddenly I heard all this muttering and sputtering at my back. There were passengers stalled on the steps and passengers jammed in the aisle, not a one budging. Where was the bottleneck? I couldn't see it.

No help for it but to order the passengers back down off the steps and elbow my way inside.

"¿Qué quiere ella?" a female voice was shrilling.

The cause of it all wasn't far to seek: this elderly lady who wanted to sit in the front row. As, I must add, she was fully entitled to do. The front two seats, right behind the driver's, are priority seating for seniors and handicapped. Only problem was that a gal from Mexico with a kid had settled in there first. The old dame was standing on her rights, refusing to budge; she'd started reading aloud from the sign under the window ledge, which stated in no uncertain terms exactly who had first dibs on these seats. The Mexican was waving tickets in her face, shouting something about having bought good tickets with "mucha lana"— plenty of money—and being able to prove it.

"Pagué al contado. ¡Mira! ¡Aquí está la prueba!"

So I stepped in, doing my best to explain the obvious: "I don't think she understands English."

"Then maybe she should pick another country!" The old lady's voice was rising. She was quite a sight, dressed for a tea party or church or something. Nylons, heels, gloves—the works. Normally—and it turned out to be the case for her—anybody dressing up is bound for a short journey. So you had to wonder: was it worth all the fuss?

"Now, ladies," I said.

"¡Tengo la prueba!"—the other was still waving her proof of a ticket. "¡Mira!"—look!—thrusting it furiously; and then, wouldn't you know, the kid was climbing on her neck, clinging, starting to squall. I had maybe three dozen words of Spanish; none of them terrifically apropos. "Por favor," I started, but all I could manage after that was "bas— bastante," enough what? and "muy amable," very kind. I made small tamping-down motions with my right hand, doing my best to let her know that her ticket had been noted, it was OK, she had proven, she could put her proof away now.

"You know . . ." I turned to the standing woman, making an effort not to get ruffled, touching her elbow gently so she'd lift her head, stretch her gaze a little. "There's a seat ready and waiting for you right over there, and I'm sure the nice lady sitting there"—I pointed, taking my chances—"would be glad of your company."

Unexpectedly, I'd lucked out. The nice lady proved to be so, signaling "over here—right over here!"

It was fourth row back—only a few steps more—yet the woman who'd started the ruckus was far from pacified: "Shows what this country is coming to!" she announced to the rest of the bus. Her voice was shaking. All we needed was a back-and-forth on this subject, but thankfully nobody took her up on it.

And she did settle down at last, though not before extracting a piece of tissue from her purse and dusting off the seat. Her seatmate offered a few soothing sounds for which, once again, I was grateful. We weren't completely over it, though. The Spanish-speaking gal in priority seating was now in tears. My next job should have been trying to calm her down, but I'd had it with both ladies, and I didn't even try. Talk about the U.S. of A. as the great melting pot! That's the official story, what we'd *like* to think, but you've got to wonder. Call this *melting*?

Anyway, by then the blockage was cleared, the line was free to move. We were back in business. I returned my attention to those waiting, and soon I was face-to-face with the girl I mentioned. That dress should have told me, if nothing else. And then her ticket gave Hunters Junction as her destination—so I knew I was right: she had to be the same one. I felt obliged to remind her that it had been a special detour, my stopping at Hunters Junction before; this time, she'd have to transfer in Stanton for the last leg of her trip. She answered in a wispy voice, "Oh, sure, I know."

So she was going back . . . It had been a dead-end move. A little over five months between then and now, not all that long, really. And yet she'd aged—years for months, it looked to me—something had aged her. But I didn't have time to wonder much before turning to the next customer.

After

DIDN'T MEAN A THING, THE TINY BROWN FINGERS GRASPING her dad's thumb like that. A reflex was all. But Dee Anna couldn't help staring. The old lady sitting beside her kept on crooning, "There, there . . . It's all right," full of advice nobody was asking for, when even Dee Anna had enough sense to think twice before telling black people what they ought to do. But this lady never once hesitated. Try rocking the baby, she suggested for a start. Not working? Try a little milk. No? How about sugar water? Never heard of a baby that didn't like sugar . . . Then maybe it's gas, it's usually gas. Turning her over on her stomach and rubbing her back should help. In circles, that's the way. No better? Why not give the pacifier another try? Won't take it? She's a stubborn one, all right. Are her feet warm enough, you think? . . . Well, then how about ignoring the baby, hard as that might be, for a minute or two? Nothing wrong with a good cry—it fortifies the lungs. Now the baby was furious, knotting herself into a tight bundle, pumping her fists, revving up to yell her lungs out.

Dee Anna couldn't stop staring at them, the holy threesome across the aisle. Sure, they were frustrated, yet bound up in a love so thick and sweet they were sticky with it. *Even blacks had more than she had* . . . She felt a stab thinking this, so quick-sharp a stitch in the ribs she had to turn away. Had to catch her breath. Forced herself to focus on the stubbled back side of the seat ahead of her: *Feast on that!* Hard to believe it was plush once, velvety . . . She didn't want to look out the window because they were speeding now, racing full tilt down a hill, it felt like falling, and she thought, *Before long I'll be back in Hunters Junction—how can I face them?* and *I can't! I must!* Houses and signposts flew past, dwindling to specks, to nothings. Snatched away, leaving not a trace . . .

She hadn't said good-bye to anyone.

Still at it—the baby sputtering, her tiny legs in the pink-spotted tights battering her dad's chest. Her dad was trying to interest her in the pacifier again, but she kept spitting it out. And he kept rescuing the thing before it tumbled off the edge of the seat, finally giving up and stashing it in his shirt pocket. *Now what?* The baby continued squirming. Dee Anna's seatmate seemed to have used up all her advice; she was saying not a word.

Now the mom and dad were thinking that changing the baby might do the trick. The mom rummaged in the bag at her feet, coming up with a fresh diaper and some powder. Cooing, stroking, the two of them expertly lifted and tucked, the dad making funny faces all the while. The baby went right on fretting. One last go—with big gestures the baby couldn't miss, her dad stuffing the pacifier into his own mouth. At this the baby hushed. The pacifier was bright blue with a smiling Mickey Mouse on the outside. Mickey was upside down. Her dad's lips curled around the thing, smiling at how ridiculous he must look, and the baby stared, eyes wide in wonderment, growing quieter and quieter as she gazed. Then her mom started up, chanting, "Whad'ya see, girl? Whad'ya see?"

Dee Anna, wrapping herself in her own arms, wished for meds, a blanket. A blindfold, maybe. She kept worrying the fabric of her dress, plucking it away from her skin. She'd been doing this so often for months now that she was no longer aware of it.

She was chilled through and through. Could have said something to the driver about turning the heat up, but it wasn't for her to say. If the lady sitting next to her, who'd had an opinion on everything else going on, wasn't going to say pip about it, then maybe it wasn't the air temperature at fault. Dee Anna hadn't felt anything like normal for a long time, especially after yesterday morning, holding the bundle to herself that one and only time. How warm that was, how warming . . .

A nurse carried the baby in, wrapped in a white blanket, fast asleep and smelling all over of milk. Whose milk? Dee Anna knew that it wasn't by accident that the baby was sleeping: in the nursery, they'd made sure she'd been fully fed before bringing her down. All that was left for Dee Anna to do was to hold her, rock her a little, and stare at her face for the few minutes allowed.

Only when the nurse stepped out for a second did Dee Anna dare to unwrap the blanket and pry loose the tiny hands and feet. She was cupping both feet lightly in the palm of one hand when, suddenly, they'd kicked free. And then, in a heartbeat, the nurse was back, standing between them. It was much too soon—and already too late: the peach-fuzzed head had turned to face Dee Anna, their eyes met, the baby's swimming, not yet keyed in, and her tiny fingers had curled over Dee Anna's forefinger. *Hello and good-bye . . .* The baby had to be pulled from her arms. She knew, sure, that the baby's fingers holding on to her like that didn't mean a thing; it was nothing personal—a reflex, they'd fasten on anything. Dee Anna knew that. But her head turning, their eyes meeting—did that mean nothing? Nothing at all?

Remember me . . .

Some of the girls had asked for blindfolds in the delivery room. Everyone advised against holding the baby; they said it would

hurt all the more. That much was true. They said that seeing the baby would make it harder to start over, to move on, to
forget. True and false: it would be harder to move on and she
would never, ever forget. They told her that she'd made a mistake
and paid for it. She was going to do the loving, the responsible,
the unselfish—the *only* thing to do. She was going to put her
child first. The baby was so tiny, so weak, how could she—Dee
Anna—hope to protect her? There were people waiting to give
the baby security, a better life, a real family to grow up with. A
mom who could afford to stay home for the baby. A dad who
cared. A beautiful home with a room set aside for the baby, a
nursery stuffed with toys, a swing set and sandbox in the yard—a
yard big enough for all that. "More than you could ever dream of
giving her," they said.

They said: "You can't give *those* things but you can give a beautiful gift."

The baby's name—Dee Anna knew it wouldn't be kept—
was Claire. The papers were signed the day she held the baby,
their only time together after the delivery. That was yesterday—
so hard to believe that was only yesterday! The baby was now
"award of the court." Weren't those the words they used? Dee
Anna didn't ask what "award of the court" meant. If she asked
dumb questions, her baby would go to a family low on the list, so
Dee Anna asked no questions. Besides—there was this terrific
pressure, everybody was in such a rush to get this thing over with.
"For *your* sake," they kept saying. Over, done, finished—but how
could it ever be finished? "Speak up, please," the judge urged her,
but Dee Anna could not lift her voice. "Are you certain you have
no questions?" he asked one last time. Dee Anna shook her head:
No. No questions.

She'd given the beautiful gift.

The baby across the aisle seemed to be sleeping at last, and the
lady sitting beside Dee Anna had turned to other things—her
watch, for starters. She kept putting it to her ear and giving her
wrist a shake. It was one of those teeny-tiny fancy watches ladies

wore for dress up. Little dots for numbers, real dainty, but hard to see. Dee Anna knew and dreaded what was coming, the prying sure to follow. Any second now . . .

And there it was: "Would you happen to have the time?" the lady asked. This was just a warm-up, Dee Anna felt sure.

"No, ma'am, I sure don't." Dee Anna's toes were clenching, but nobody else could know that. Worse yet, she caught her hand gravitating, seeking to keep in touch with the empty place. She managed to turn it away in the nick of time, but the minute she quit thinking about the one hand, both hands started to drift forward and—it was like they had lives of their own—came to rest on that same place.

No use. Dee Anna could actually *feel* the stare of the lady beside her, the beam, the slow burn of her attention—curiosity? concern?—focusing on her. There was nothing else close at hand now. The baby across the way was sound asleep, so the old lady needed another topic of conversation. Dee Anna knew full well what was coming.

As expected: "If you nap too early, you won't be able to sleep through the night," she began. "But maybe you're not traveling that far? . . ."

"No, ma'am, I mean—yes'm, partway," Dee Anna answered politely. Oh, yes, she was in for it.

"By the way, my name is Eileen Brinnin. You can call me Eileen." She went on to say that she was from Chickasha, Oklahoma, and made a great point to Dee Anna of how the name of the town was pronounced different from how it was spelled. It was called Chicka-*shay*. "And you're . . . ?" she asked.

"Dee Anna, ma'am."

"Like the princess?"

"Not hardly, ma'am. Nothing to do with princess."

"Lovely girl," Eileen said softly, almost to herself. "I don't care what anybody says. Can't be easy being a princess—everybody on your back all the time, snooping . . ."

"Yes'm," Dee Anna said, to be saying something.

"How time flies . . . ," the lady seemed to be thinking aloud. "Why . . . Seems like only yesterday that Billy, my youngest, was that size . . ." She thumbed across the aisle where the baby lay stretched out, head nestled in her mom's lap, feet brushing her dad's thigh. "Seems like only yesterday," she said again, "but you're too young to appreciate . . ."

Dee Anna sort of hummed, something that sounded like, "um . . . uhuh," to show she was awake and listening.

"You think it's lasting forever when they're cranky or colicky, but it's only a little minute—then, *whoosh*, you're a granny and it's all over . . ." The lady seemed to know that she was talking mainly to herself, her voice trailing away then finding itself again. Now she was going on about how she wished she'd taken her crocheting out of her suitcase instead of stowing it in freight, it would have kept her hands occupied at least. And how much she'd looked forward to teaching one of her daughters or daughters-in-law to make lace, but not a one of them cared to learn; they didn't have the time—neither the time nor the patience—for it.

Dee Anna tried to picture meeting Claire fifteen or twenty years down this same road. Traveling on this same bus, could be. Maybe even, by coincidence, both of them happening to sit side by side. Of course, her name wouldn't be Claire then . . . Would Dee Anna recognize her? Or would they spend the time chatting about timetables and weather, as strangers do, never once guessing there was anything more between them? Wouldn't something be bound to show? Maybe she'd have Dee Anna's eyes or the same gap between her two front teeth? Something—wouldn't it?—would surely tip them off . . .

"I'd say you were all of sixteen, yourself," Eileen put in.

"Seventeen," Dee Anna corrected. She lied with conviction now. In fact, she was fifteen, and that barely, but she'd always been big for her age.

Dee Anna had been warned, plenty, about lies. How the Lord felt about lying, first of all. An abomination with its own special hot seat in hell. How people went crazy when they told lies, you didn't have to wait for hell. But this lady—this Ellie or Eileen—had to be stopped someway.

"Seventeen," Eileen mused, "wonderful age"—but whatever she was about to say next was lost as they pitched forward. The bus shuddered to a near standstill. To Dee Anna, the distraction seemed heaven sent.

Congestion ahead: cars mincing along single file. Soon the bottleneck was upon them: a van with flags, trailing two flatbeds, each with half a house aboard and signs that warned WIDE LOAD.

"Will you get a look at that? They just pick up a house, saw it in half, and put it down someplace else, maybe three states away . . ." This old lady loved stating the obvious. "Seems to be nothing we can't do these days, if only we put our minds to it."

On and on and on. "When I was your age . . ." Up front, the Spanish-speaking woman was telling a story to her little boy, "y de aquel día en adelante, el grillo . . ." Dee Anna tried to fasten onto that, and to what she guessed were cricket noises, the "chuchuch chch!" that followed, but the old lady beside her kept droning, drowning out the other voices. This, then that . . . An uncle who drank. A cousin who died. A trait that ran in the family. Her youngest grandson's favorite joke. The weather back then, and now. The things that were wrong with the world now. The things that were still all right. When she finally gave up the effort, she sat, head bowed, staring at her ruined hands with their knobby joints, their backs mapped with what looked like coffee splatters. She stared longest at her rings, fingering the plain gold one, adjusting the sparkly one to catch the light. It seemed to Dee Anna that all the old ladies she'd ever met did that very thing, must spend hours staring at their rings. She, Dee Anna, would never do that. Would never *have* that.

All Connections
Open Wide

"WHEN I WAS YOUR AGE . . ." EILEEN KEPT COMING BACK TO
this. She knew that her young neighbor wasn't listening. They
never did listen, the young, no more than she herself could have
been bothered to pay attention at that age.

Something else . . . It struck her that the girl was coming from
someplace she couldn't imagine, where being young meant something she couldn't begin to imagine . . . Something about her
dress, the primness of it, the plain collarless neck, the particular
tucks and gathers around bodice and hips, the skirt falling a good
ten inches below her knees . . . Where in the world had she gotten
that dress? Probably hand sewn—it looked almost homespun—
Amish, maybe. But the only Amish girls Eileen had seen seemed
happy, unaccountably happy. They wore bonnets. And they never
traveled alone. So that wasn't it.

Now the girl, staring dead ahead and blinking, was fighting
back tears, she was almost sure. Eileen had done all she could do
to keep from putting her arm around her and pulling her close,
saying something foolish like, "What are shoulders for? . . . Here

I am beside you, honey. Use me." But the girl leaned away as if she felt the tug of Eileen's intention and was determined to stay clear of it.

So Eileen herself pulled back a bit, biding her time. There wasn't anything else to tune in to—except for two women loudly broadcasting their misfortunes: one allergic to wheat, milk, cats, cleaning sprays, even Band-Aids gave her blisters; the other, arthritis, her heart climbing stairs, her "calciferous" heart.

Their competition was cheerful and friendly enough. And all too familiar. What Eileen liked to call the "outdoing of diseases" seemed to be a favorite pastime of people in their latter years. Although Eileen had her share of aches and pains, she refused to join in and play along.

All in all, Eileen had enjoyed good company up till now. Across the aisle, where the colored couple with the baby was sitting, there'd been another, older pair traveling to their granddaughter's wedding, marveling—with the bride nearing forty—that they'd lived long enough to see the day. *Perfectly lovely people . . .*

And there'd been the young woman married a year, returning to her husband in St. Louis. She'd been so friendly. "Am I doing the right thing, you think?" she kept asking. They'd had their first big blowup and she'd fled. Eileen tried to play it safe at first with, "You're the only one who knows for sure," but then couldn't resist moralizing a little. "How you happen to feel at any particular moment is the least of it," she said. And more—about commitment. If marriage meant anything, it was a promise made, this was her conviction. The young woman was still riding with them—same bus, but she'd moved elsewhere, hoping, she explained, to find a little more leg room. Come to think of it, she'd done a lot of seat changing since . . . *What was her name? . . . Started with* R, Eileen recollected.

Eileen had to admit she was getting weary, though—there comes a point. She'd boarded the bus only this morning and already felt like she'd been cooped up for days. Normally—until a few months ago, to be exact—she would have made a trip like this by car, but she'd been scammed the last time she'd driven alone, and Gary, her eldest, had begged her not to give him ulcers by risking worse the next time. Having nothing but time on her hands, she'd obliged him. So here she was now, bored witless. The wind glistened on the other side of the glass, but she couldn't feel it; the passing scenery could as well have been some kind of blurry film unspooling, none of it real.

Eileen thought of herself as shuttling between deathwatches, even though her first visit wasn't exactly a death, and despite the fact that she'd managed a layover with a cousin in Wheeler, before setting out again, this time to Paulette, her sister-in-law, in Evanston, Illinois. Evanston would be the real thing, though in slow motion. Paulette had months yet to go, was enjoying life even now, so much so, in fact, that she'd asked Eileen to bring along one of her wonderful poppy-seed cakes.

The cake, inside a plastic container—the container, in turn, well cushioned by crumpled newspaper—was hidden in the hat-box under her seat. It was Eileen's only piece of carry-on luggage. Little could happen to it, short of a traffic accident; nonetheless, she kept tapping the box with her heel to make sure it was still there. It was a grand cake, if she did say so herself. The finest ingredients, she'd stinted on nothing for this one: fresh eggs, butter and milk from the Landon farm, and she'd soaked the poppy seeds in scalded milk overnight. Then, everything mixed, she'd added a touch—just a smidge—of lemon zest.

Eileen's first stop this round of visits had been down in Texas—in Pampa—to help pack her aunt Margaret off to a nursing home. Eileen hadn't been looking forward to this at all, in fact she'd been girding herself up for battle, as she frankly admitted to anyone who asked. Margaret was over ninety and was rumored (although it turned out not to be the case) to have pretty much stopped eating. The old woman had been saying things like, "It's enough. I've enjoyed just about all I can tolerate," and one of the young sprouts in Pampa had called Eileen to report this as a clear signal that Aunt Margaret had made up her mind to quit living forthwith. Eileen wanted to say, "That happens, that's her privilege." Problem was, the habit of living was hard to break after so many years. The old woman's heart was still strong. And the point was . . . What was the point? Eileen's thoughts kept circling away and back . . . Oh, yes, it was the fact of its being pretty much the same journey again and again lately, packing up for someone's last move or a sickbed, that made Eileen think of these trips to Pampa and Evanston as one and the same.

If she'd been driving now, she might feel a bit brighter about things. What she missed most of all about driving was the freedom to stop whenever, wherever, she pleased. Like right this minute how she would have loved to crack open the window and let in some air . . .

"You ought to rest," her kids kept urging her, "you've earned it." Rest from what? she wanted to know. Rest *for* what?

Soon maybe, she'd have to give up driving altogether, she knew that. Eventually, her absentmindedness would begin to take its toll. How often of late had she started to pull away from the gas pump with the hose still attached to the car? . . . Only a matter of time. Till then, she'd hold on as long as she could, driving short distances; then: only in town, to the grocery and the library. To church and the beauty shop, for reasons of habit, though beauty operators couldn't do much for her these days. What, for that matter, had she left to cling to after all her years of churchgoing? Nothing grand, surely, the barest of bones for a creed: to live in hope. And even that so sorely tested . . . Anyway, the long and the short of it was she'd given in at last to her children's objections. There would be no more long drives. Her old Buick, bought fourteen years ago, had seen over a hundred and fifty thousand miles and better days. The problem with long distance, *one* of the problems, was that all she knew about cars was little more than skin deep; what went on under the hood remained a mystery to her. That's why Gary had put his foot down about her driving this time and, she never denied it, the reason she'd been taken advantage of during her last trip. Fact was, she couldn't tell a tie-rod from a tonsil. Long ago, she'd learned to rely on others for what she didn't know. Was that really so foolish?

To be entirely truthful, though, Eileen had to admit this wasn't the *only* reason she'd been singled out. Eileen had always been too trusting, she knew that. Sometimes—but more rarely than Gary would have it—her trust was misplaced. Be that as it may, she'd rather be too trusting than the other way around. Still, Eileen knew better than to argue with Gary, or with any of her children. She didn't blame them. They lived in a different world now, less friendly than the one she'd inhabited, more dangerous altogether.

So she'd been deceived, she'd been had. She was turning in at a self-service Texaco when the young man signaled her to a halt. He had a "pleasant face"—when questioned afterward, she couldn't get more particular about him than that. "Clean-looking fellow in new jeans and a pressed shirt." "Soft spoken, nice smile."

"I hate to break this to you, ma'am," he said, and he did sound sorry to have to bring it up, "but your tie-rod's about to drop off." When Eileen ignored him, he repeated himself, louder this time, and when she blurted out, "My *what?*"—she'd grasped this much by now—he knew she'd swallowed his bait. He beamed, "This is your lucky day." He happened to be a mechanic on holiday, or—how did he put it with that sidewise smile of his?—"a mechanic on the loose?" And he was all solicitude for her safety. "I don't like to even *think* what will happen when it drops," he said. So she'd moved her car over to a deserted corner of the parking lot, well away from the traffic at the gas pumps, as he'd directed her, and she'd thrown down an old towel for him to lie on. Then he hauled himself under the belly of the car and, except for his neatly turned jean legs splayed out on the pavement, all but vanished. She could hear him grunting from time to time as he settled into his struggle with whatever it was he was after. Eileen couldn't help noticing his running shoes. She recalled them more clearly than his face, having seen more of them. They seemed to be new and—though she was no judge—expensive. Even the soles were decorated. The neat yellow zigzags looked like light-ning streaks.

Eventually the legs heaved. With a sharp cry, the torso—the neck—the young man in his entirety—raised up, a tiny pin cupped in his palm.

"See this!" He wanted Eileen to see. With an expression of utter disgust, he held the thing out to her, as if that frail bent wire was all that held the tie-rod in place, all that kept the car in one piece. He'd already explained how the tie-rod's job was to hold the front tires together, and had even taken the time to draw a diagram for her. "Talk about shoddy workmanship!"—it never had been joined right.

He'd saved her life—so, of course, she'd paid him. Nearly all she had on her: thirty dollars for the emergency service and twenty more (her second-to-last twenty) for his new baby about to arrive "any minute now." And when he repeated that it was her lucky day because she'd run into him, she believed him. They both smiled then (for different reasons, she realized later) as he wished her "Safe travels!" and waved her on her way . . .

Yes, *of course,* she ought to have known better.

But at least you couldn't fault him for enterprise and cunning. He'd even had the temerity to write up a bill of sale for services rendered. She could still recall the receipt, recite it like a poem, word for word:

> Tie-rod pull adjust
> due to overlube of boot
> boot split, lube leaked down
> Pin popped out
> All connections open wide

When Eileen tried to describe the operation to Al, her mechanic back home, she presented him with this receipt. All Al could do was shake his head. "What some folks won't do!" he said, biting back a smile. "Did it look like this—the pin he pulled out?"

Eileen nodded, "That's it." It looked like a tiny hairpin. "This is a cotter pin," Al explained. "Know how much this little sucker costs? Let me see . . . Could it be more than a nickel?"

So that was what it amounted to: a single cotter pin. Heaving and grunting, the young man had slipped a cotter pin out from somewhere underneath the car, or from his own sleeve, maybe, and then, with more heaving and grunting, he'd popped the pin back into its original place. There'd been nothing wrong with her tie-rod, nothing at all wrong with her car. She'd been duped.

Eileen was old enough to know better, experienced enough to have noticed all the little giveaway details: his pressed shirt, his hands too clean and unscarred for those of a working mechanic. And, what ought to have been most telling, he'd been far too eager to help. So all right, sure, she should have known better. Even so, when all was said and done—allowing for an occasional swindle—she didn't think "all connections open wide" was such a bad way to be.

Anyway, it was thanks to that rascal that Eileen was now traveling by bus; he was to blame for her being bored out of her skull, growing stiffer and more restless by the minute.

But maybe there was some relief in sight, they seemed to be heading for the exit ramp. Another town, another stop. At least she'd be able to stand and stretch in place, even if they weren't allowed to step off the bus.

It came up so suddenly. Before Eileen knew it, they were at the station, aiming for one of the numbered stalls, where a small crowd was already waiting. The driver made a poor joke—pathetic, really—about not stopping to pick up this new batch of customers. "Looks like a bunch of losers," he announced. *As if they looked any different from the passengers already on board!*

"How about we turn around," he added, "and leave 'em here?"

And almost in the same breath came a shout from the back of the bus: "*Do* it!"

On the Move

WHAT'S WITH THIS CELEBRITY BUSINESS? . . . ANYTHING *to be singled out, to be seen—therefore, to exist.* Sam Shevra couldn't help but marvel at it. *To be monstrous, even, but to exist.* No telling how many crimes reported on the evening news were caused by a craving for fame, any kind of fame. Carried by solitaries, nourished by crowds, the infection was everywhere. Here, too, of course.

Case in point: the lady tattoo artist from Flagstaff who'd kept Sam company through the long desolation of the Texas Panhandle. She boasted of having tattooed old-fashioned stocking seams up and down the backs of her legs from ankle to butt; she'd been the first person known to have ever done such a thing, and they'd written her up in a national magazine. Would he care to see her work? Sam assured her that wouldn't be necessary, but she was a flasher, and he got to see it all. After that, there'd been the country music wannabe, an affable, acne-spotted youngster, on fire to give the world what it never knew was missing; he'd dialed 1-800-BE-A-STAR and, after a brief detour for funds in Oklahoma City, would be on his way again, glory bound for Nashville.

Now, as his new seatmate settled in, apparently intent on a nap, Sam hoped for silence, a needed respite. A chance to open a book he'd brought along, give it yet another try. The book, *Eat the Rich,* a semi-serious economics primer, never held Sam for more than a few flickering minutes, though he kept at it, stopping and starting over. Not that it wasn't diverting—it was altogether too diverting, crackling with pungent anecdotes and one-liner wit, but Sam couldn't determine what the thesis was or where the mathematics were to be found in support of any. The author's attitude seemed to be, "Screw the math, we're reader friendly here." Impatient to grasp the general drift at least, Sam fast-forwarded to the last few pages, only to learn that, overall, in a free-market setup, the rich got richer and the poor got richer (albeit by ever so little, and slowly), and everybody got older. It wasn't really an interruption when the napping passenger stirred and started to strike up a conversation. "Nice title," he observed.

"It's not what you think," Sam warned.

"I used to read ..." he sounded actually wistful, "not anymore ..." Except for talking a blue streak once started, this man proved to be better company than most. Sam realized belatedly that he wasn't likely to find a traveling companion as sane and agreeable again.

Sam's apprehensions were well founded, for the next passenger to settle in beside him turned out to be the craziest of the lot: a balding, middle-aged man on his way to Indianapolis with a load of inside info he was aching to disgorge. The lowdown on everything: how the concentration camps were faked, and the moonwalk was a made-for-television movie, shot in the Nevada desert. Sam had heard the moonwalk story before, the exact same, note for note; for all he knew it might be a regular feature of bus travel.

"They sure put a big one over on us there . . . bunch of lies," he went on, "just like that mushroom cloud." That, too, was a special-effects spectacular, straight out of Hollywood.

"Bet you never heard any of this, and guess why"—it wasn't a question. "None of it ever got reported. People tell me I oughta write a book."

"You ought. Make a million, I bet," said Sam.

The man nodded; apparently he'd been told this before. "You don't think I'm serious," he replied.

What next? The Trilateral Commission's covert control of everything, including weather, menstruation, and tides? As intelligence declined, volubility increased. The instant the seat up front emptied, Sam hustled forward to claim it, throwing down his jacket to stake his claim, then threading his way back down the aisle to gather his overhead luggage. He'd had his eye on this particular seat for a long time—ever since he boarded the bus in Laughlin, in fact. "Angel seat," he'd heard somebody call it. It was on a sort of platform, making it higher than all the other seats, including the driver's. With its wide, unobstructed window, it had the best view in the house.

Resettled, Sam directed his gaze out the window and studied the waiting throng. Maybe it was his temperament, a certain detachment natural to him, reinforced by his schooling, being tracked early on for science, which led him to think of people in the aggregate first, and then only after that, almost reluctantly, of the individual case. His bent was for generalization and, observing the larval swarming of the passengers at the gate, he couldn't help but generalize now, reflecting on how compliant, how orderly by comparison, airplane passengers were. The demon word *class* leapt to mind. Sam did his best to dismiss it: Americans did not believe in class. *Could be a question of trust,* Sam reflected (coming round to the same thought by another route), affluence and trust, the two went together; plane passengers could afford a more benign view of other people: for them, the system worked. But as for present company, these wasters (the driver had said it, not he) jostling for position at the boarding gate—the system was failing, or had already failed; they had to elbow and shove just to keep from being swept under.

And here he was among them.

Next time, Sam promised himself, he'd fly. Granted, even with a price war, there wasn't an airline in the business that could beat Greyhound's fifty-nine- and sixty-nine-dollar specials, but the extra expense would be worth it. He needed to leap clear of the human mess, craved the cleanness of liftoff. Thirty thousand feet up everything's calm, everything's nice. A little flattened maybe, but nice. But this grinding along inch by inch, nose to the ground, was grinding Sam down as well; he was mired in too much close detail.

Feeling the crawl of sweat under his collar, his familiar jitters starting up, Sam loosened his top button. Time for a little attitude adjustment—a brightener. His fingers rooted around in his shirt pocket, ferreting. *Not there? It had to be there! But, no, the big one, the Paxil, the pink pill for blue mornings, was surely gone*—he must have taken it on schedule. Obviously it hadn't worked. What he had left were two aspirins and the miniature squeeze bottle—artificial tears for dry eyes. So much was artificial lately . . . Half the time, he couldn't tell whether he was hungry or not . . .

But where was his Ativan? He needed something to smooth him out. The mere thought of losing his Ativan made him frantic. *No, wait, there it was, hiding in the seam*—the pill was so miniscule. He really could get by without it at this stage, he knew that. He *could*—but why sweat it? The uncertainties were bound to catch up with him the closer he came to his destination. He was no hero—why court anxiety? And tossing his head back, Sam swallowed the thing dry.

There. Done. Bound to be better. While folding his glasses into the same pocket, Sam's face took on the wobbly, underwater look of the severely nearsighted. He sighed, stretched, leaned back. Recited a little mantra he'd devised for himself: "There's loneliness, there's isolation, there's sealed in stone . . ." He was simply lonely, it wasn't that serious yet. A wee bit down was all, low to midrange of the spectrum, nothing heartrending so far. And wasn't it better to be alone as he was now than to keep the kind of company he had for the past—how many hours?

HAND THEM A MICROPHONE AND MOST OF THE DRIVERS are hams. Some of them have regular comedy routines and a need to make their particular personalities known. I flattered myself that that wasn't my case, but there were times I'd say a thing, pretty much anything, to get a rise out of people, times I got carried away. Like calling that bunch of passengers waiting to board "losers." But what *got* me was the way they lined up for boarding. Every single time! It wasn't so much an outright pushing and shoving, more an edging themselves forward, but it came to the same thing. If I told them to line up on the left-hand side of the door, they'd be sure to edge to the right, distrusting the official word on everything, convinced I was hiding something from them, cheating them out of some advantage free and clear to everybody else.

Anyhoo . . . We were on our way, the old 8213 unexpectedly peppy on the uptake. We'd see how she handled a couple of hundred miles down the pike . . . I picked up the microphone and introduced myself again, this time giving them the full spiel. I always tried to lighten things up if I could. I guess you could call that hamming. "You all know who you are?" I started. "Can you swear to it?" That fetched a few laughs. "I'll tell you one thing," I went on, "you're all going in the right direction, heading east to find fame and fortune." On the way back, I'd make that "heading west to find fame and fortune." In point of fact, they were the walking wounded, all too many of them, on the move because the dream crashed—the job folded, the rent was overdue, the car got repossessed, the casting call never came.

I gave them a quick rundown on rest stops and transfer points, and the usual about behaving themselves. Gave my first, last, and final warning: no booze, wacky tobacky, or silly powder; no radio or tape deck played without a headset. Federal regulations about no smoking on board. The nice-guy bit about trying to accommodate smokers by giving them a few short stops that weren't on the menu, but only if—two big *ifs*—everybody behaved themselves and let me make up time.

"Restroom for your convenience . . ." And so on and so forth.

"So put your seats back, your heads back, relax, and behave yourselves, and we'll try to make up lost time." It was an old

All That Road GOING

script—except for the lost time and the different stops for different schedules. My standard closing: "If you have any questions,
or you're too hot or too cold, I don't want any hollering from the
back of the bus. Haul yourselves up here—carefully—and tell me
about it and I'll do what I can. Everything clear? . . . Got any
questions?"

There were no questions.

Minute I switched off the mike there was a burst of applause,
then a hoot or two, the usual funhouse yipping and yapping, coming—no surprise—from the back of the bus. Deciding to ignore
them for the time being, I shed my cap and we were off, main-
streaming down the highway.

A lot was familiar on this trip so far. Like the old lady who
started me off this run by raising a ruckus over priority seating.
I'd dealt with her kind on a regular basis. Legally, she had every
right, but she was so much better off where she ended up. Seemed
to have found a soul mate in her seatmate, so to speak; they'd been
head-to-head ever since I placed them together.

Not so for that ghost of a girl from Hunters Junction, who
looked pretty squirmy where she was sitting. The lady she was
sitting with was one of those talkers. Been dishing out free advice,
right and left, ever since I'd come aboard. I bet she hadn't a clue
as to the girl's story. Maybe that's why she kept hammering away
at it.

Like I said, I've seen a few.

After all the years I'd put in there wasn't anything much, short
of a broken axle, that could give me much of a jolt. Certain excite-
ments, I must admit, had grown old—even working the extra
board, getting the call two hours in advance telling me to go to
wherever, never knowing beforehand where or when. Crossing
state lines had grown so routine I hardly noticed anymore. And a
hundred-mile cup of coffee, black as tar, didn't go the whole way
like it use to, didn't give me the same lift, nor did pearly lipped
Angelina at the Blue Sky Café in Jay City, though plenty of older
drivers still flocked to her, laughing over the same stale jokes as

if for the first time. I'd heard pretty much all that could be said in favor of the old Silversides buses, rulers of the road before my time, overlooking the fact that they had no PA systems, no power steering, and no restrooms.

All that gassing over the good old days! It's a theme song by now. Over and over—how the quality's gone down, the clientele "isn't what it use to be." Too many shiftless, jobless, or quitters around. "They want the money, but they don't want the work." Dropouts, druggies, welfare moms, name your pet peeve. Too many people with larcenous hearts wanting something for nothing. Not much different, really, from those CEOs with their tax cushions and loopholes, living off us honest drudges . . . And what do *we* get? Taxes, more taxes, never a break. "Crick in the back, a retirement watch . . ."

They have a point.

I don't know . . . Every now and then I'd think of doing something else. Driving a tour bus, maybe. If only charters paid better, I might do more than toy with the idea. Tours appealed to me: the passengers all getting along—singing, sharing, it *should* be possible—since they're all going to one and the same place with pretty much the same ideas why. Little like pilgrimages in the olden days. I wouldn't mind Carlsbad Caverns—or Graceland or Six Flags, or just about any theme park or capital city. And driving night or day wouldn't make that much of a difference with the place so known. Seemed to me like it would be a lot easier than what I had to put up with.

But there wasn't that much to complain of right at the moment, and not that much traffic, most of it holding to an orderly seventy, seventy-five. Until a couple of horse trailers pushing sixty came into view and an ancient, mud-spattered pickup, hauling a round bale on a spike and hugging the forty-five minimum.

No sooner had I put the hay bale behind me than I was up against one of those Harley caravans trying to blow everybody else off the road. The crew was decked out in black—black leather jackets and jeans, black boots and saddlebags. No helmets, of course. *Of course.* A few wore bandannas, pirate fashion. The only other relief from all that blackness, if you could call it relief, was the chrome of their chains and gizmos, metal catching sun from behind them. I had to pass, get shut of them. So I burned rubber . . .

Big burst of speed, keep it up, keep it up . . .

Generations

EILEEN'S VOICE TRAILED AWAY. WHEN SHE'D MENTIONED
her kids to Dee Anna and added, "they all married well," she
knew the minute the words were out of her mouth that it was the
exact wrong thing to say. Resolving to ease up on the girl, she
turned her attention elsewhere.

Across the aisle, the baby was sleeping peacefully at last. The
parents—Eileen reminded herself they were supposed to be called
blacks now, not Negroes, not coloreds, even though they weren't at
all black, the man was more mahogany, the woman mustard—were
talking heatedly. Eileen could catch most of what they were saying,
but it was clearly none of her business, so she eavesdropped as they
debated whether or not their journey had been a wasted effort. Had
it been worth disrupting the baby's schedule? She'd be cranky for
days. Here they'd traveled over six hundred miles to show the baby
to her great-grandmother Felice—she'd been named Alanna for
Felice's own sister—and the woman hadn't wanted to touch or even
look at the baby. They'd contrived to take a photo of all of them
together, the two of them positioned behind Felice's wheelchair,

with the baby more or less suspended over her great-grandmother's head. "Maybe," Alanna's mother speculated, "there simply comes a time when a person grows weary of the whole bother of generations." Felice was well up in her nineties, after all. And it wasn't as if they hadn't been warned beforehand how bitter and forgetful she'd become. So—had the trip been worth it? They went round and round that question. The father wasn't at all convinced. The mother was. The main thing, she insisted, was that all the time and trouble it cost them proved that *they*, at least, cared. And Alanna would do just fine, regardless of whether her great grandmother cared or not, it wasn't a judgment on the baby. Alanna didn't need anyone else's approval to get on with her life . . .

Eileen, tuning in and out, kept firmly to her resolve not to enter into any more discussions uninvited. And to leave her seating companion alone, even though Eileen knew, anyone could tell, the girl was aching. Even so. Eileen could do nothing but keep her hands to herself, her mouth clapped shut. To offer nothing. Here she was with all the mileage of eighty-five years behind her, all that experience, surely good for something, but, no, nothing—*nothing's usable*. She might as well be shut up in a box. In a way, she was.

She did her utmost to shift her attention to the passing view but found little to hold her interest for long: a field of new green; a fallow pasture; another field, freshly furrowed; a grain elevator; a creek bed, rusted dry. Those splurts of coppery red in the distance turned out to be cattle. The scenery changed, but her thoughts continued to circle round the same fixed point: the girl beside her. The girl wasn't simply silent but . . . How to put it? Muted. Fiercely muted, if you could say such a thing.

This was one little person who badly needed cherishing, Eileen felt sure. Problem was, now that the girl was in easy reach of comfort, she was liable to bolt from it. And why should she trust Eileen, a perfect stranger?

Now the girl was fidgeting in her seat, lifting the hair off her neck as though she were sweltering, and hugging herself as though she were cold. So which was it, cold or hot? And she kept on tugging at her dress, pick-picking at the blouse part. It was then Eileen thought she saw something. It made her wonder: a damp spot, no, maybe just a shadow where, strange . . . a tinge, a faint smudge . . . But how could that be? The girl was too young. Besides, she wasn't carrying anything.

So preciously young . . . A wayside town flickered past, then a long stretch of leave-out land; the girl shifted restlessly in her seat, never managing comfort. Eileen caught herself in a drowse, her head starting to dip. Then they were passing a pond, which broke the monotony a little. "Wish I could paint that," Eileen murmured softly. She couldn't help herself.

Dee Anna half turned to see but found nothing of beauty in the scene. Only a ragged pasture with something thrown down in the middle of it: a watery rug. The late sun struck a few muddy gleams from its surface. *Mud, dreaming light.*

"So pretty . . . They say water is the hardest thing to paint," Eileen blundered on. She simply couldn't contain herself a minute longer. "I don't know . . ." She turned to the girl as if Dee Anna might have some opinion on this, which of course she didn't. Eileen was talking to herself and, as usual, couldn't stop once started. "But then, if I ever tried to paint that pond," she went on, "I'd have to write *water* all over it to let people know what it was supposed to be."

Dee Anna had nothing to say to any of this. She could have been looking at wood, stone, leaf litter, rain—it made no difference.

Why even bother trying *to talk across the generations?* Eileen thought. They might be different tribes, different species, the young and the old, for all they had in common . . .

Eileen suspected she was the oldest person on the bus. If eighty-five wasn't old, what was? She wondered about the lady who'd raised all that fuss about priority seating. She'd appeared to be in her mid-seventies, at most, and still agile. As it turned out, she'd only been traveling a few stops up the road. And she'd gone off so quietly (When? Minutes ago? A half hour ago?) that Eileen hadn't noticed her leaving. The Spanish-speaking lady she'd tangled with had also quietly disappeared. So what had all that fuss been about? And where had the energy for it come from—a woman in her seventies?

"We're like melons," Aunt Margaret used to say. "Cut from the vine, we don't get any sweeter—just squishier." And, oh yes, another one of her famous remarks on the subject: "The nails thicken, the skin thins. We don't improve over the years—or the centuries, for that matter."

Aunt Margaret's mind had been sharp as a tack. Right up until this year.

Even during this last visit, there were glimmers, moments when Eileen couldn't help but believe that it was all there still, memory and wit, like a water table under dry earth. Like what she'd said about that man on death row . . .

They'd been listening to the six o'clock news. The big story was on Flint Revelson, who'd been on death row for twelve years, who'd killed, raped, and never repented, and who was due to be executed by lethal injection that night. The new news was that he'd made the longest menu request for a last supper on record. Four hamburgers with all the extras, double fries with plenty of ketchup, three chocolate milkshakes, a pint of fresh strawberries with a pint of whip cream. And that wasn't the half of it—he'd asked for a whole slew of brand-name candies, M&M's and such, to top it all off. The final straw as far as the prison officials were concerned, though, was his asking for fresh strawberries. There they'd balked. Frozen, maybe, but fresh? Out of the question!

The entire menu had infuriated Eileen. "Boy," she said, "if that doesn't take gall! 'In-your-face,' as the kids say."

But Aunt Margaret wouldn't agree. "He's telling us he's still in love with life," she insisted. Why had she been so emphatic on this? By way of letting Eileen know that (despite all reports to the contrary) her old aunt was still in love with life, as well?

She'd do that, Aunt Margaret. You'd think she was clear out of it—off the planet—and then she'd startle you with a comeback like that.

Other times, she couldn't find the right words for anything, like *pizza* for Peter. And *hugs and kisses* were "huskies." She was alert enough to know that these words weren't quite what she wanted; coming out with them a little cloud of disappointment would cast its shadow over her face, her eyes would mist.

When Eileen was summoned to help Aunt Margaret break up her house, she couldn't help thinking of it as a rehearsal for what would be coming in her own life. If she lived long enough, that is . . .

It was unnerving, how a lifetime of slow gathering took only days to disperse. Most of Aunt Margaret's furniture had gone to the Salvation Army. The bridge table and folding chairs would go there, too, at the very last. The special pieces, like the antique breakfront, the piano, and the cedar chest, had been dispatched to one or another of the grandchildren.

The remainder—the love seat, the low rocker with cross-stitched morning glories on the cushions, and the small cabinet Margaret's father had made for her as a child—were on their way to her single room at Clearview Nursing Home.

There were only a few items that Margaret couldn't decide on, like a carved wooden cane they'd found, brocaded with dust, in a forgotten corner of the attic. It had a twist-off handle with a knife inside. Aunt Margaret claimed to have no idea whose it was or how she'd ended up with such a thing. It was no joke: the edge of the blade was still razor sharp.

Sorting old letters proved a harder job, letters and sepia-toned newspaper clippings, crumbling from brittleness when unfolded. She'd been a clipper and hoarder much of her life, Margaret admitted, but tended to be going to the other extreme now. "Seems like my work is mostly tearing things up these days," she observed. Together Eileen and she pored over announcements of weddings and obituaries. Of prizes—4-H, the best strawberry pie in the tristate fair, some girl in the family making it to the county spelling bee, where the word that defeated her was . . . The word was chipped away.

All That Road GOING

After that came the photographs. "I might forget a name," Aunt Margaret said, "but I never forget a face." It was heartbreaking, really. So many nameless photos, so much grist for the leaf-and-lawn bag. Even with the pictures of her own children, Margaret was just as likely to call out the names of her grandchildren.

It was more than a little scary. Lately, Eileen had caught herself doing the same thing, her mind spinning through the roll call of generations in search of the right name. Some names were recycled, so there were fewer to recall than faces, and Eileen, too, recognized most of the faces even when she fumbled the names.

Desperate for prompts and footholds, Eileen tried putting particular talents to faces. She pointed to Allie and Glee in one of the photos; all she wanted was for Aunt Margaret to confirm the names so they could label the photograph and send it on to the right person. But, here again, they clashed. Aunt Margaret claimed that Glee was the one who sang and it was Allie who played the piano, while Eileen was equally adamant that it was the other way around. Finally, Aunt Margaret cut her off, objecting, "Why does everyone have to have a talent? That's something I never did understand. Isn't it enough to be a nice person?"

You couldn't win. Many of the photos were discarded without ceremony or comment. Sure, it was heartbreaking when you thought about it. Better not to think.

Yet how could you avoid either—thinking or sadness? And returning to the present, here it was: more heartbreak, right beside her. Old age had no monopoly on this, and Eileen felt sorrow coming at her, wave after wave, as she turned to the young girl sitting next to her. The girl seemed no more comfortable with being left to the privacy of her thoughts than she'd been with their conversation before, since the restless fidgeting and plucking at her blouse had continued just the same. So Eileen decided there was no further point in keeping silent. At the very least, talking would help make the time pass for both of them.

And so Eileen plunged. There was a tremor flickering through her hands and neck (she could feel it, and the girl probably noticed it) from so much bottled-up resolve so suddenly upended.

"Going far?" she started.

"A ways." The girl wasn't making it any easier.

"Going or coming?" Eileen persisted.

"Both," the girl answered, her face flaming. She seemed stung by the least question. But why? She'd revealed nothing. Diana—or Dee Anna, rather, the country version—could have been a fake name, of course. But what could she possibly have to hide?

Eileen didn't know where to go from here, and the silence thickened between them once more. She turned away from the girl then and studied her lap, her hands crossed idly there. There were no distractions to be had now: the parents across the aisle were drowsing, the baby, deeply asleep, stretched across both their laps.

Maybe the girl wasn't so unusual, despite her dress. At fifteen, sixteen, hadn't Eileen's own daughters and granddaughters clammed up like this? Her daughter Laurie was barely fourteen when she began to insist on her privacy, resenting what she called Eileen's "snooping into everything."

And yet, with this girl, Eileen sensed there was something more to it. She was different—*damaged somehow*. Or, no . . . *Wounded* would be a kinder way of putting it.

And it was this new word come to mind that made Eileen persist—this, and her never-outgrown schoolteacher's habit of pushing at people, youngsters especially. She was interested in people was all. Since when was that a crime?

Eileen was just about to start up again when, abruptly, the girl lurched to her feet, clutching her stomach.

"Scuse me . . . Got to . . ." She was already in the aisle.

"Let me know if you need anything . . ." Eileen called after her, but the girl was no longer staggering, she was moving swiftly, purposefully, down the aisle.

Yes . . . Something wounded there, Eileen reflected. *Wounded, famished, something . . .*

Cutting Loose

DEE ANNA NEEDED FOR PEOPLE TO STOP—SHE HAD TO get away.

But there was no air inside the restroom; the place was stifling, a space for toilet and sink no bigger than a broom closet; no window, unless the keyhole counted. And it must of been over a wheel, she could feel the wheel turning. Just thinking about that turning tired her out. The old lady she'd been sitting with tired her out; she'd acted like there was some sort of connection between the two of them. *What connection could there possibly be?* They just happened to be thrown together for a few hours, like all the other strangers on this bus.

Checking her blouse in the mirror, Dee Anna was relieved to find it dry and clean. Only maybe one little damp spot, hardly noticeable unless you were really on the lookout for it. Although they'd given her a drug to keep her milk from coming in, Dee Anna didn't trust it, she was afraid of spotting. She was still bleeding, but that went on in secret. It was less than yesterday; she knew it was to be expected.

A moment of privacy at last . . . And it did help, she did feel a little bit calmer.

Then a tapping at the door ruined it.

"Hey . . . you in there."

Her time was up.

Getting free of her seating partner had clarified one thing for Dee Anna: there was no way she was going back into that situation. *No way*—the old lady was far too curious. The trick would be to find someplace in the back of the bus that was clean and private.

The first opening she noticed was next to a man with a knit cap pulled over his ears. He had a lunch box on his lap, the enameled metal kind that kids in the elementary grades tote to school, but his was a plain black one without any cartoon animals or goofy flower faces. The fat sausage of his duffel bag sat beside him, taking up a full seat for itself. The man didn't look like much of a conversationalist, which was fine by her—it would be a relief. But she had to ask twice, "Anybody sitting with you?" and, even then, had no idea whether he'd heard her. She asked a third time, doing her best to project her voice: "Excuse me, is this seat taken?"

But she might as well have been talking to the duffel bag: the man stared dead ahead, not an eyelash fluttered. Dee Anna didn't believe for one minute that he was deaf, though maybe he really couldn't hear her with his ears stuffed up in that cap of his, and who knew what he had under the cap. Besides, she'd just noticed the strong unwashed odor coming from him, not a bit inviting. So why bother?

The only other free seat she could see was next to another man. He looked sort of old. Could be forty, she thought. Older was safer, wasn't it? Dee Anna told herself that she had no choice: it was either the snoopy old lady she'd been sitting with or this man. Men were so little curious—about people, anyway—that he'd probably leave her alone. Another good thing: if she did decide to sit with him, she'd have the aisle seat; if he started acting fresh, she could easily escape.

So Dee Anna put the question to him. When he returned a puzzled look, she pointed to the empty seat, then to herself. He studied the motion of her hand carefully, then asked, "Is not too . . . How say you?" and brought his hands close together. Dee Anna said, "Plenty room. If you don't mind." He drew up his knees, scrunching closer to the window, murmuring something in reply, some thick word Dee Anna had never heard the like of. This seemed to be a clear enough yes, and she settled in.

Dee Anna had felt the old lady's gaze trailing after her as she fled down the aisle and could see her head swiveling from time to time, seeking her out even now.

Well, she'd catch on eventually. Dee Anna knew she was being unfair. The woman wasn't simply nosy, she was concerned, she meant well. *Oh, more than well. But spare me*, Dee Anna thought, *spare me your concern.* All she wanted was to be left alone.

Which was pretty much what was happening here. For it soon became clear that Dee Anna and her new neighbor were walled up in different languages. He did have a couple of books on him, and every few minutes he'd open one, running his finger over the letters, giving a soft, rustling cough, then glancing sidewise at Dee Anna, as if gearing up to speak. Like a man tuning an instrument, almost ready.

Finally, he did speak: "How say you this?" and pointed to something in his book. The word was *gosh: "My gosh! She's playing with fire."* He passed the book over to Dee Anna.

On the left-hand pages were words of a strange language, even the letters were unrecognizable to Dee Anna. The words in bolder print on the right-hand pages were in English:

> Golly, that has a strong fragrance!
> May I kiss the bride?
> It's a team sport.
> I have no quarrel with that.

Dee Anna had to wonder: when had she heard anyone ever say *golly?* Still, it wasn't her place to be correcting the instruction book. She mouthed the word for him, repeating it twice before handing the book back.

"But, please . . ." he said, setting the book aside and scratching around for his ticket. It was one of those computer-printed ones, thick with folds, a complicated journey.

"What means this? And this?" He pointed to the words *arr* and *dep.* Earlier, in the half darkness, the man seemed old, but under the light of the reading lamp, he appeared much younger. Dee Anna noticed he was wearing a gold ring, which maybe meant something or maybe not; she knew better than to trust it.

Before she had a chance to learn his final destination or where he'd started from, he'd tucked the ticket back in his pocket. Then he stooped to rummage in the shopping bag under his feet, bringing up a sack of chips, which he pushed toward her with scooping hand gestures and "Please—my pleasure," urging her to dig in. She thanked him, shaking her head no, at a loss to explain how chips made her thirsty. He looked so disappointed, though, that Dee Anna felt she had to say something more. "But that mustn't stop you from eating—*you* eat," she insisted.

"Is OK?" he asked. "For certain?"

"Please," Dee Anna assured him.

So he polished off two handfuls, crunching quietly, almost apologetically.

Not long after, there was a brief stop that wasn't on the schedule. A reward for good behavior, the driver announced. Dee Anna's seatmate hurried away, carrying a small plastic kit. Dee Anna had no plans for stepping out—*what for?* She wasn't even interested enough to ask what place this was. There was nothing out there that she needed. She wasn't hungry or thirsty, she'd already been to the restroom. And something else kept her rooted to the spot: she had no desire to go past her old seatmate. Nor did she want to pass by the black couple with the baby. Man and wife were sleeping now, the woman's head resting on her husband's shoulder, his head curved in toward hers. *Even blacks had more than she had . . .* Dee Anna tilted her seat back as far as it would go and tried her best to think of nothing at all. After only a few minutes, her new seatmate returned, his hair wet-combed and flattened; he brought with him the smell of minty aftershave. It struck Dee Anna that he looked almost Chinese with his dark hair slicked back and his high cheekbones. And something about his eyes . . . They were sort of slanting. Maybe, too, it was his politeness; that's all she knew about the Chinese, slant eyes, quiet, and polite. Oh, and yellow skin, of course. But you couldn't really tell in the feeble glow of the reading light. Then he switched off the light and stretched toward the window, propping his head smack up against the glass and seemed to be out. Seemed to be—you never could be sure. Dee Anna, for her part, remained wakeful and watchful.

Hard to believe it was only five months since she'd been put on this bus. Felt like it happened in another life. And now she was going back to Hunters Junction the way she'd come. But why? Because the return ticket had been given to her and was already paid for; because she had no money of her own. Because she'd been so lost up till now that when anyone called her by name she was likely to go in that direction. Though no one was calling her name now . . . But still—what else was there? Born, raised, schooled, and churched in Hunters Junction, she knew no other place.

The morning they'd sent her away was etched clear in her mind. Her stepmom holding tight to Dee Anna's arm to show her support, or maybe to keep her from bolting. The other three ladies from the prayer chain at Blazing Victory Apostolic Church standing alongside, trying to make conversation. Dee Anna numb, just plain numb, she could have been brain dead at that point, the fact that her eyes were watering didn't mean a thing. She was dazed by the light of day, the clear, cutting light. Cooped up in the house all summer long and into the fall, creeping from room to room, drawing shades as she passed, she'd grown unused to daylight, unused to other people. Her stepbrother Luke was back with his unit at Fort Leonard Wood—she'd given daily thanks for that.

Dee Anna had waited, standing outside the doughnut shop that doubled as a bus station, surrounded by her stepmom and three other ladies, and it seemed like they had so much concern, they'd given so much thought to her situation, while Dee Anna couldn't think at all. And she couldn't begin to grasp what was in store for her. All she could do was to stare blankly ahead. There was a boy, sitting on a curb, eating a sandwich. There was a squirrel. Dee Anna couldn't remember why she'd been staring at them or why the picture they made together kept coming back to her. The baby was just floating then, not yet heavy, not yet real. The church ladies did what they could to comfort her best they knew how; they spoke their kindest words: she'd have time to think after this, time to repent, to mend her ways, amend, wipe her slate clean. She'd be able to start over, a fresh start.

Dee Anna had no idea what lay ahead, of how she'd still be cooped up for months to come, how slow it would be, doing time with so many other bad girls, girls whose full names she'd never be permitted to know.

The girls came from as far away as Kansas to Sheila's House, named for some Sheila who'd once been in trouble herself and had gone on to evangelize, saving "hundreds and thousands of souls." Which was a fine story in its way, though Dee Anna wondered whether Sheila ever thought back to what she'd given away. For the girls who came in Dee Anna's time, the stories were short and pretty much alike: they came, they left something, they went away. Like there were no babies. Like they'd only been dreaming babies.

Aside from their housekeeping chores and the joke of their "home-away-from-home-schooling," their only distractions were television and Sundays. The television was going most of the time, whether they were watching or not; the staff frowned on it but didn't interfere; it was a kind of riot control, Dee Anna reckoned. All through the week, they watched that endless parade of game shows, soaps, murders, romances, their eyes bleaching out on everybody else's dreams. Happy endings made them choke with laughter; they laughed to keep from breaking.

And there were Sundays. The preacher who came to them should have been two preachers. Sometimes he'd be pale and pinched—it was the way he held himself—sometimes rounder and ruddier, gesturing with palms flung out, arms sweeping wide. From week to week, you never knew which preacher would show up; the message, from one Sunday to the next, meaningless, the words so pleated with dark and light, with kindness and meanness.

But maybe, Dee Anna came to think, *it was all an act, a way of playing out the bad cop, good cop routine to keep the girls in line.* Among themselves, they'd named the pair Mr. Blue and Sweet Satisfaction—the Worm and the Apple.

Mr. Blue was the harsh one. "*Fornication*—an ugly word!" he'd say, his lips parched on it as if he could taste the word and it was poison. But they all knew how much he enjoyed saying it—he said it so often. How their only hope was to be "plucked from the burning." Whenever he got started on this, Dee Anna would pluck at the skin on the back of her hand, making the veins stand up. It was only a little painful; it felt real—and it was something to do. His rant was old: how they'd heaped shame on themselves and their innocent families, had muddied and bloodied the words of Holy Scripture, and were already ticketed, express bound, for hell. Unless—unless, there was still a window of opportunity!— they fell on their knees and called upon the name of the Lord. One by one, they would have to come to the Lord. On their knees. The Day of Judgment was near. How he welcomed the dawning of that day!

"Beware of sin: it bites, it bites, is never fed . . ."

Sweet Satisfaction sang a different tune, but why would anybody believe him? What were the most powerful words in scripture? "Jesus wept." And what should that say to them? They'd suffered and sorrowed and God understood. *God weeps!* Hearts were broken to be reshaped, re-formed, redeemed through suffering and sorrow. "Jesus said: 'Neither do I condemn thee.' And

Jesus," he was happy to report, "said that in red!" But the girls couldn't swallow this line either. Problem was they all knew that Jesus had said a whole bunch of other things, also in red, that were far from friendly.

By and large, they preferred Mr. Blue to mealymouthed Sweet Satisfaction. Mr. Blue at least was a straight shooter. Most of the girls at Sheila's House took pride in living up to their reputations for being bold and brazen. If Mr. Blue expected weeping and wailing and gnashing of teeth at his words, he was wildly mistaken. His rants only hardened their hearts the more. If they were bound for holy hell, then to hell with heaven! "Let's go down with a blast!" was the attitude. And when Mr. Blue declared that they had only to look at themselves to behold how fallen a world it was, Susan's face flamed. She coughed, and the girl sitting beside her thumped her on the back, though everyone knew that her cough was a sham, a cover, and Susan bursting—having to hold in, wanting to shout out.

Dee Anna would not open the Bible she'd brought with her, though she knew that words of consolation could be found there. They were only words. Her mood zigzagged from sorrow to anger to sorrow.

She remembered Susan, full of sass, griping through her ninth month as she twisted and turned through the night, trying to find a comfortable position. That was Susan before. Then, after she'd come back from the hospital, her last night at Sheila's House, how strangely mute, how still she lay. She wasn't sleeping. Dee Anna's bed was closest: she could catch the glitter in Susan's eyes whenever the light of a passing car swept over the ceiling. Susan was awake, her eyes were shiny, wide open. When Dee Anna reached out her hand to rattle Susan's bedpost, it was like knocking at the door for permission to enter. But Susan's head did not turn. All Dee Anna could do was to take back her hand and whisper, "Does it still hurt?" Not a word. Susan drew up the sheet, covering her whole face with it—the only reply.

Dee Anna understood when her own turn came.

Hands strapped to the sides of the table, heels caught in the high stirrups, knees forced apart, with full light blaring down, exposing the place of her shame for all to see, Dee Anna avoided the doctor's eyes, as he did hers. She was thinking that she should have asked for a blindfold when the nurse kindly plopped a pillow on her chest, cutting off half her view.

Nothing about it had been natural. The labor had been—how did they call it, *induced?*—that was the new word she'd had to look up. It occurred to Dee Anna that the baby's official birthday would never be her real one, it would be the day they forced it. Dee Anna had really been due later this week, but the doctor, or somebody else important, had to be out of town on the due date, it wasn't convenient. Dee Anna had raised no objection; by then, all she wanted was for it to be over.

She'd been told to shower and get ready to leave Sheila's House for the county hospital. Dee Anna still didn't feel she had any real choice but to do as she was told. Nobody ever took the time to tell her what induced labor was like. Instead of the cramping and loosening up she'd expected, it had been steady, grinding pain—hours of it—with no breathing spaces, no letup.

She'd only just glimpsed the baby in the delivery room— so wrinkled and ancient looking and streaked with blood. Dee Anna couldn't raise herself up enough to see properly. "Boy or girl?" she had to ask. The doctor said nothing, and it was the nurse who answered, "Oh, a girl. A nice one." Then the baby was whisked away.

And that was when they knocked her out—*after* all the pain. When Dee Anna woke, she was doped up on Valium and whatever else it was they gave you to keep your milk from coming in. Either she didn't know what she felt or she no longer felt anything at all. They'd put her in a bed with a curtain round it so she wouldn't be able to see when the babies were brought in to the other mothers—the real mothers—to be nursed. Dee Anna never complained; she thought her good behavior would make things easier for the baby.

It made her clench up now when she remembered: how soon after that the adoption papers were brought in. She had to sign them before leaving the hospital. There'd be a period after the signing when she could still change her mind, but how could she change her mind if signing the baby over was, as she'd been told again and again, the loving, the mature, the only responsible thing to do?

Only once had she tried to question things: "And where do you plan to live?" the social worker asked, "since your mother has made her wishes crystal clear." And when Dee Anna remained silent: "How do you intend to support yourself? Do you think you can strap an infant on your back and find a paying job? And, supposing you could, did you ever think how that would be for the baby? Do you plan on buying a crib for her? Or letting her sleep in a cardboard carton or a dresser drawer? Don't you want the baby to *thrive*?" On and on like that.

The social worker, or whoever she was, kept on asking questions about the father, too. Dee Anna had enough sense to lie about him. "An older man," she told the woman. And she'd made up a name for him, a name that belonged to no one she'd ever known: Len Fuller. "He was professional," she thought to add. At the word *professional*, Dee Anna noticed the social worker pause in her note taking. "Oh," the woman asked with an overly pleasant smile, touching the pen to her lips, "what profession might that be?"

If Dee Anna told the truth, her baby would go to a family low on the lists. "Manager," she improvised. "I met him on my after-school job at Allsups." This wasn't a lie. The sales manager had flirted with her on the job but never after working hours. "He was already married," Dee Anna added. This, too, was fact.

She would not give the real father's name. They couldn't force her.

The truth was another story altogether. Jimmy, best buddy of her stepbrother Luke, was the one. Luke had put Jimmy up to it—

a dare, she felt sure, some kind of joke, for the heck of it. Her secret hideout down by Miller's Pond hadn't been so secret after all.

It happened so fast . . .

. . . Hands tore, clutching at grass. He emptied his sickness into her, threatened if she screamed—how could she scream gagging—*no air?* Warning her if she told, "Don't you ever, don't you ever . . ." Scuttering away like a crab.

She hadn't screamed, she never told, who'd believe her if she tried? And after minutes?—hours?—hadn't dared to move but to cover herself. Shivering in the warm. Drenched, after astounding heat. Such a lovely day! Feathery clouds, leaves, everything spangled with sun. And no one. Nothing cared. Her raised hand trembled, scribbling the air. Around her, ants, tiny mites, fleeing for their lives, struggled through stalks and tangles, forests of grass. Getting away—for now.

Dee Anna couldn't help questioning—had she brought what happened upon herself? Had she hidden away hoping to be rescued? To be found?

When she stood up, it was dizzying. Had to hunch back down quick, pressing her knuckles into the ground to steady herself. She squatted to pee. Her pee was dark tinged, scalding.

What she had to do was to find a hideaway deep inside herself, deep in the cave of her mind, where no one from outside could find her, not even the people she thought she knew. She didn't know.

So why go back to them?

Her ticket was punched for Hunters Junction, the only reason. Where else could she go?

She'd lost everything. Lost feeling as surely as she'd lost the baby. Had to numb herself—no way of getting through it if she hadn't. Yet whenever anyone told her that she'd "forget and move on with the rest of your life," she knew it was a lie. She wouldn't forget the chill of the metal instruments, her swollen belly the shelf they rested on. Would remember forever that first and last meeting, the baby's head turning, eyes swimming to meet her own.

But—she wasn't entitled, wasn't fit; the baby had to be protected from her. And whenever Dee Anna reminded herself of these facts, she was relieved that the baby had not been misshapen, considering how messed up a mother.

Teenage was over; barely begun and already she'd died to it. Her stepmom had pulled her out of school, out of everything, even before she'd begun showing. Her dad had raised no objection, shrugging it off as women's business. Now her stepmom would be counting on her help in the house, what with Kaydie not yet three and another of her own on the way. *Let her cope!* It was none of Dee Anna's concern.

Too late now to even think of returning to school. There'd be no way for her to catch up—she'd missed so much. If she started over in the fall, she'd be a whole year behind. She couldn't face anyone she knew. Couldn't wrap herself in prayer and never mind their stares. Couldn't pray—*who to?* Couldn't face her pastor; Brother Lyle was the one who'd made the arrangements for Sheila's House. He was sure to be keeping his eye on her. By now, everyone in Hunters Junction knew. She could just hear them . . .

But what to do? She couldn't think what else, couldn't get her mind around any kind of future. Couldn't hardly believe she was still here, one and the same person, in a continuing life.

All she could feel was the empty place inside her. She'd been hollowed out to make room, more room, and the hollow remained. At Sheila's House, her feet puffed, her ankles swelled, she'd been stretched and stretched, her skin too tight—and now so loose it felt like she'd put on somebody else's coat, no longer her own skin. Before the kicking started, she'd floated, nothing—the baby least of all—had been real to her. But looked at another way, thinking back on then and now, it must have been a thick, rich time; she'd been rooted then, connected, even if she hadn't known it, the baby hers, all hers, still knotted to her.

Columns, Arches, Dreams

"THINK I MADE THE RIGHT DECISION?" ROBERTA ASKED.
Her neighbor, an older woman with poofy (probably dyed) auburn hair and dark lips, said something about "muddling through" and "marriage is no bed of roses." She'd already told her her name but Roberta had been too busy—caught up in her own story—to listen and felt it would be impolite to ask her to repeat it.

Then the woman asked, "What was your big blowup about?"

So Roberta told her how she'd been slaving away all day, dead on her feet from work, then shopping for food, cooking a special supper for the two of them, lamb chops, cream potatoes, and apple crisps, and then having to set the meal aside, let it go cold and dry, while she sat there on a slow burn, eating nothing, burning up, she hurt so bad. Until he finally showed up at three in the morning, never having bothered to call or even dream up an alibi. "I was pretty well pissed by then," she concluded.

"An understatement, I bet," her companion offered.

"And jealous, of course . . ."

"So you run off and leave him to her?"

"So I run off to have my own adventure. Always wanted to see California. And I almost did. If he hadn't had me paged in Tucson . . . Got my ticket switched in Tucson and turned right around . . ."

"Right around his little finger, sounds to me," the woman put in. "You should of gone all the way while you were at it. To Santa Monica or Venice Beach. Get your toes in the water at least while you were at it. I hope you didn't apologize."

"Why would I apologize?"

"You'd be surprised: women do. Tell me this—did he apologize?"

"You've been married, I guess . . ."

"Don't ask," the woman said.

This sort of killed off conversation for a while. Roberta turned in upon herself then and let herself have it. Why did she need to keep blabbing on and on about Robert? To make him real? *Wasn't he real?*

In silence, Roberta fished a comb out of her handbag and worked over her hair with slow strokes, it steadied her. Then she got busy with her compact, snapping it open, angling the little mirror to the light. With a practiced finger and a dab of spit, she adjusted her kiss curls. She noticed that her left eyebrow needed tweezing—it was higher than her right and gave her a criticizing look—but the bus was too bumpy to risk trying to even things out right then. Her nerves were shot—all the stress she'd been through—and she had no idea how to occupy herself except talking. If nothing else, it was a way of killing time.

"Like to see my wedding picture?" she ventured.

"Sure," the woman said, "why not?"

It was black and white, a three-by-five Roberta had laminated for handling. She'd been keeping it in her purse, taking it out from time to time, mooning over it in private.

For a long moment, the woman studied the picture. More silence—Roberta couldn't stand it. She leaned over the woman's shoulder, straining to see herself and Robert in another's light, the cool, distancing light of a stranger's gaze.

But the woman remained tight lipped. She saw two youngsters, the man tall, stiff, with big feet, and big hands poking from his sleeves, clearly unaccustomed to his fine clothes. Jug ears. And his Adam's apple gawked. Looked like he'd had too much party and gobbled the cork.

"That's him . . . Pretty handsome, right?" Roberta prompted.

Her neighbor nodded: "Hmm."

"He's six foot four, but his basketball days are over. Varsity, I mean. He still plays for the fun of it.

"And that's me, of course . . ."

"That's a nice dress," the woman said.

"Better believe it! Know how much it cost?" Roberta named the price.

The woman, sucking in her breath, seemed properly shocked.

"Only live once, right? Everybody kept saying it. 'This is your big day. Princess for a day.' Stuff like that. So I had it made exactly like I wanted—organza lace and a sweetheart neck and a bodice fitted so tight I couldn't hardly breathe. Little bustle in the back you can't see here . . ."

"And what's this?" the woman asked. She pointed to the columns and arches in the background and the fountain twined with bunches of sculpted grapes. "Where were you?"

"Dreamland . . . Castles in Spain, I suppose," Roberta replied. "Almost fooled you, didn't it? But it's only a photographer's setup. Trying to look more romantic than anyplace in Missouri . . ."

"It sure looks romantic."

"And it was," Roberta sighed, "it was so incredibly awesome."

Can't live in dreamland forever . . . Roberta was no fool. she knew there was a lot she'd have to face when she got back to St. Louis. Finding a new job, for starters. She'd been so sure she was leaving for good when she set out, so steamed, that she'd blown off a perfectly good job without giving notice, without even bothering to call in sick. *I'll show him*—was all she could think of at that point. How she'd given him everything she had and he'd treated her like nothing. Like a piece of shit. Kept her up all night waiting and worrying, all but choking on rage, because he couldn't be bothered to pick up a phone. And now she wondered: had she come around too easy? All he'd had to do was page her, and without a moment's hesitation, she'd turned right around and come trotting back to him. He had her eating out of his hand. He was her whole life, and sometimes she wished she'd never laid eyes on him—how could this be?

Why was everything so slow? They needed to talk.

Despite everything, Roberta couldn't hardly wait. In the days between her running away and coming back, it was like the whole earth, the very air, had changed.

When she set out, seemed like everything around her was holding its breath. Sky—a dull metal casing, tamped down tight like a lid. Tight, shaky buds.

But once she'd turned! Everything started to breathe, to shimmer. The air suddenly adazzle. New leaves all over, soft as feathers. The change, she realized, was partly her mood. But partly the season, too, moment by moment more deeply into spring.

Spring or no spring, the closer she got to St. Louis the harder it was to wait. She was dying to be back in his arms, she loved him so bad. And she knew he loved her, couldn't get along without her. Why else have her paged in Tucson? Tucson settled it. Yet her thoughts, circling, would not settle, would not be still. It was like some salt lick of the mind. Or like that game her mother taught her—he loves me, he loves me not, plucking the petals off daisies till only the bare button-hearts remained. The answer almost never came out the same two times in a row, nothing sealed it, there was no peace, no rest, no end to it, you had to do it over, again and again, forever shredding.

He made her almost hate herself . . .

And yet—and yet—last night, late, passing houses with lights undimmed, she'd catch the shadow traces of heads or hands behind drawn shades. Shadows only, but they'd burned into her, left bright stains in after-image, filled her with such yearning that she *knew:* a love so strong could not go unanswered.

It had to be so.

Two

Threads

IT TOUCHED EVERYTHING HE SAW, AS THOUGH THE GLASS had a hairline crack across it from edge to edge of the frame. Like a thread stuck to a camera lens, the same thread—he couldn't blink away the thought—spooling through Marie's fingers, taunting him, the thread that wasn't there . . .

Pierson stood up and extricated himself from his jacket, placing it tenderly, lining-side out, on the overhead rack. Fortunately, the overhead was empty—his seatmate had only the one small valise he was using as a footrest. Resettling, Pierson played with the arm lever, trying to find the most comfortable, then the least uncomfortable, angle, coming back round to the same position he'd been in, seat in mid-recline, left leg crossed over his right. It would have to do.

At last, pretending to sleep, he did sleep, though fitfully, in spasms. His dreams were troubling, full of urgent instruction in a language he did not know.

What could he reassemble on waking? Images only, scraps: the white stalk of a throat, the open mouth of a fish, a dog in a tunnel, a face (human) bursting out of a sleeve. A needle darting, an arrow aimed. Stiff fingers laboring—*but this was no dream!*—adding stitch to invisible stitch . . .

What was joined in this stitching?

Nothing so far, nothing to nothing. Pierson's eyes blinked open.

The man in the next seat turned to greet him. "Had a good nap?" he asked.

"So-so," Pierson replied, his voice thick with sleep. Felt like he'd dragged himself back from someplace far, far away. Had no desire to return there. But now the man was taking out his wallet. Here, wouldn't you know it, came the photos: the wife; the kids; the family at Christmas; the son in his first football uniform, first set of pads; the trip to Disneyland . . .

"And you?"

"Always forget to take them along," Pierson mumbled. "I mean to but forget."

"You must of been married a long time."

"Long time," Pierson agreed.

"Kids?"

Pierson shook his head.

"That's too bad. Can't remember ever wanting kids before they came along, but now I couldn't call it a life without 'em. Of course, they're a helluva lot of trouble from day one, and once they hit the teens all bets are off. Don't know if I can stand it . . ."

"Guess I'm still at your first stage," Pierson said. "Hard to miss what you've never known." And then, lacking the energy to cook up a story, he added, "My wife is sick. Very sick."

"That right? Sorry to hear it. And you're on your way to her?"

Pierson's answer was oddly truthful: "She's expecting me," he said.

Almost night . . . Up ahead, a lighted billboard proclaimed:

"JUDGE THE LION BY THE PAW"

Some paw! Some lion! The church alongside was nothing but a great big shack, unsteepled, with a mangled roof. Tilted, leaning away from the sign, it looked about ready to crumble into the ground.

Another sign:

PRAYER STILL PRACTICED HERE

Then church and placards were swept behind them.

What Pierson said about not having kids wasn't exactly true . . . Wasn't exactly untrue, either. He'd had a kid once—Kenny— from his first marriage. Hadn't laid eyes on him since the kid was a couple months old, looking like any other puling infant that age. Truth was, Pierson didn't know how to think of Kenny. As an ex-kid? Or what? Funny . . . how the language had no words for this. If alive, Kenny would be a dad by now. Dad—or granddad, even . . . But neither possibility was real for Pierson since Kenny remained unreal to him. He'd been trapped into marrying the kid's mother, the whole situation a kind of blackmail.

The driver seemed to pick up speed as darkness came on. It was dizzying. Buildings blew by, smeared together. Same way drunkenness smeared things, though Pierson was stone-cold sober now. He could get off at the next stop if he chose to, he reminded himself. He could still turn back. Thinking this, he couldn't help it—it was like question and answer—he stamped his foot.

"Gone to sleep on you, I bet," his seatmate observed. "All this sitting's bound to get us in the end. Fat on the heart—number-one killer . . ."

Pierson nodded, hoping to get the man off his back, then shut him out by shutting his eyes again. He had no idea where he was going. Wherever, whatever, it made no difference. His ticket was for cross-country: a See America pass. Any place would do, there was nothing he wanted to see, no place he wanted to go, only—to be gone, to be going. Away. Not to be *there*.

Realms of Gold

"ACCIDENTALLY ON PURPOSE, YOU MEAN!" TWO WOMEN IN
the midsection were arguing.

"Look who's talking! Before you're sure, go tell, right? That's
the way you operate? . . ."

It was connect-the-dots and I couldn't. Not from way up front
in the driver's seat, anyhow. There were too many other voices
crowding in, so I couldn't catch the comeback. Another conversation had started up, left side of the aisle, close by.

". . . Upped and left and I'm never going back. Can't stand
anybody telling me what to do, telling me what to think—fucking
with my mind!"

Something—but what could anybody say?—was mumbled
in reply.

"I'll never stay put—gotta go forth. Can't let myself get stuck,
know what I mean?" No way not to know: the voice bammed on
without letup. "Don't ever look back is my policy."

"You're too damn young to have a policy," the other answered
patiently. "Go on the way you're going and you'll end up on

the street . . ." But it was useless trying to reason: soon both voices faded.

We'd just about run out of daylight. There hadn't been much of a sunset; the light cooled, a general fading. Around me, I heard the rustling of people settling, building little nests around themselves. There was the usual griping: "Been on this bus since the day before yesterday. Same damn bus! Can't get comfortable on this bus."

Most of them weren't really ready for bedtime yet, only situating themselves for the long haul. Once the dark came on, voices flared up, took over; this always happens. "Where are we now? Any idea?" They turned to ask the other passengers first and, even when I heard them loud and clear, I left them free to speculate, not bothering to step in to correct any but the wildest of wrong answers.

It was mainly the hum of talk I heard, the drone. With effort I could make out more, but I tended to tune out when the theme was familiar. Hard times, for one: "They lay you off and the stock goes up. Go figure!" Times were usually hard for my crowd.

Familiar, too, was the woman telling her neighbor, and anyone else interested, top of her voice, all her business. How she was bound for Chicago to find a job and take control of her life. *Uh-huh.* "A new start," she announced, she was turning her life around. On the right road this time. I'd heard this before. A few details were different: she'd left her four kids with their granny in California. Four kids by different fathers, she was at pains to make clear. She was in a relationship with two guys at the same time when she was raped by a third, which "kind of simplified things." Soon as she arrived she was going to call the brother in Skokie she hadn't seen in ten years—he didn't know she was coming. (I could just picture his delight.) The next thing she was going to do, once she had a job and got back on her feet, was to buy beds for the kids and send for them.

People spoke in the dark what they'd never say in the light. Even so, much of it sounded a bit scripted to me by now.

Only the guy sitting up in the front row to my right, what some call the copilot's seat and what I call the angel seat, the one on a slight step up and the picture-window view, was keeping to himself. He wasn't a new passenger; he'd started out in the back of the bus, then seized the opportunity to come forward when the seat emptied at our last stop. What he didn't know was that there was a price, an unwritten contract that came with the privilege of the picture window. The angel seat was where you hoped to put your prettiest passenger by day and your talkiest by night; drivers usually counted on the person sitting there to help keep them awake. This passenger hadn't lived up to the responsibilities of his position so far. Seemed like the effort was going to have to come all from my side. When I asked him where he was from, his answer, "here and there," wasn't too promising of a start.

But, bit by bit, I did learn a thing or two. His first name: Sam. He spelled out his last: "*S-H-E-V-R-A*." He was on an antidepressant of some kind, he told me that right off. Been down for too long, that's what got him moving. A little detour in Laughlin, he mentioned. "Guess you know how that goes . . ." I did, indeed. He didn't seem the type, though I guess everybody gets desperate sometime and, comes a point, desperate means reckless. So—Laughlin . . . Laughlin's that big casino on the Nevada border, Bullhead City right smack next to it on the Arizona side. The outfit's pure mirage, rising out of the desert with its bright blue water and palm trees. Glitter and glitz all through the night. Everything open, day or night. Giant autoplexes, hotels, motels, pawnshops. The pawnshops, anyway, are real. And Sam had been sucked in. I didn't ask how much he'd lost—thrown away. That was behind him now; he was back on course, headed on to Pittsburgh, a good deal closer to his hometown New York than Arizona, where he'd spent (pretty much wasted, I gathered) the past couple of years.

Then, sure enough, once the pump was primed, out it came— the story of his life. "It started, I guess, about four years ago . . . No, more like four and a half. I was driving with my dad through the Bronx and we were passing the cemetery where my mom's buried. Dad turned to me and said, 'Here's where I'll be, Sammy. There isn't any room left for you. You'll have to find your own place.'"

Turned out his father had died a couple of months after saying this, and Sam had set out to find his own place. "It makes a good story, I guess," he said. Wasn't quite that simple, of course; there were a couple other circumstances, what he called "precipitating factors" in his peculiar way of speaking. He'd been an industrial chemist—one of those big pharmaceutical outfits in Jersey. Then they'd started downsizing. *Right-sizing, reconfiguring* were the words they'd used. Ever since Sam had turned forty, he'd been noticing all these twenty-year-olds knocking at the door. "Eager beavers," he said bitterly, "bright eyed and bushy tailed . . . So I got shafted."

His company had no end of fancy words for what they'd done. *Voluntary termination* and *career change opportunity* were the favorites. Sure enough, management had come through with *outplacement consultation,* a neat little severance package, and plenty of leads for openings in other outfits like themselves, knowing full well that it would be the same crummy deal everywhere he called: "We'll let you know. We'll give you a buzz. We'll get back to you . . ."

Then, to make a long story short, after months of trying to shop himself around as a chemist and no sale, his credit long since maxed out, he'd landed a job in the carpet-and-upholstery-cleaning business, and it did involve a little chemistry. Once he'd learned the ropes, he decided to go into business for himself. Thought he'd do better out West, so he picked out Tempe, Arizona. He figured that rugs and slipcovers would get pretty dusty in all that dry heat, and that there wouldn't be much of a holdup for drying time. "A six-inch rain in Arizona is—what? One drop every six inches?" He'd given Arizona a go—three long years of his life. But it hadn't worked out as planned. "Like they say, Arizona is no place for amateurs." He had the drying problem licked, all right, but he hadn't factored in the fading, all that sunlight leaching color (it couldn't be put back) out of everything.

Now he thought he'd give Pittsburgh a try. The climate there was a whole lot damper than Arizona; mildew was sure to be a problem. He hadn't worked out a special process for mildew yet but hoped to once he was settled in. He'd been married, but his layoff had ended that. Right now he was single, and he didn't think that was ever likely to change. Burned once, twice shy—how did that go?

"I bet you get to hear a lot of stories," he backed off suddenly.

"Yeah, and half of them never happened," I said.

"People blown this way and that . . . ," his voice trailed away. He took out a hanky—it was far from white—and dabbed under his eyeglasses. His lenses were flat and thick as plates, and at certain angles, there seemed no eyes behind them.

I assumed that was his right name, Shevra, it was too tricky to invent, and I pretty much bought the story of his life as true—true to how he saw it, anyway—because, given the choice, he could have cooked up a better one. He was too plainly down in the dumps for me to leave well enough alone, though, so I asked him about hobbies. "Hobbies?" he echoed. Like the word was new to him. "You know, like polishing stones or petrified wood. Lot of people out West . . ." I didn't finish. "Stones?" he echoed, sounding dumbstruck. "Not stones, *necessarily*, you know, but something *like* that," I hastened to add. "It could be birdhouses." But he couldn't think of anything. Kind of sad, really: a man without family or hobbies, no outlets.

I offered him a stick of gum, but he declined. Chewing is one of my bad habits; I don't really enjoy it all that much, it's a bit of work, actually, but it's one of those things I do (part of a whole arsenal of tricks) to keep myself awake over the long stretches. And a way of gnashing my teeth when I get frustrated, I suppose. But Sam was the kind of guy who had his own opinion on every subject, even this. So, OK—you heard it here first—chewing gum, according to Sam Shevra, is "one of our national pastimes—a way of moving while sitting still." I couldn't have dreamed that one up in a million years. The truth of the matter was, I'd never given a moment's thought to what my jaws were up to.

SAM WAS AWAKE—ON STANDBY ALERT—BEHIND HIS LENSES, behind his shut lids. Although people on buses dozed off all the time, day or night, he had no intention of falling asleep now. It was way too early, and the scary part of letting yourself fall off was not knowing where you were when you woke up. That had happened to him back in the Texas Panhandle, where he'd been startled awake to find himself adrift in broad day. Outside: what should have been flyover land, vast and featureless. Far out, a grain elevator loomed like a lighthouse amid a sea of grass. Nothing but grass and sky going by. Oh, and a windmill a mile or so up the road. But the worst of it was having no internal landmarks: he'd been roused from sleep by a dark weight dragging his shoulder down, something like feathers—*hair!*—against his neck . . . a fruity fragrance . . . a woman. *But who?* He dared not move until he figured this out. What had gone on between them? He was so fuzzed, he couldn't recall a thing. And it wasn't until he noticed her hiked-up skirt that Sam recognized her as the lady with the famous tattoos.

They were high up, that was for sure: his ears were popping. Blaring. Their driver for that leg of the trip, a native Texan, fancying himself something of a history buff, had amped up the volume on his mike to deliver what sounded like a much-rehearsed tour-guide routine. They were on top of the caprock, the High Lonesome, passing through the "Llano Estacado, the dreaded Staked Plains." He spelled out *llano*—"double *l* in Spanish sounds like *y*"—as if he expected them to be taking notes.

It was here on the Llano Estacado, he wanted them to know, that Coronado's expedition had wandered in search of the fabled Seven Cities of Gold more than five hundred years ago. "Not a tree, not a shrub . . . nor anything to go by," Coronado had written, and to this, the Texan couldn't resist adding a flourish of his own: "No plow cuts, no Texaco, no Dairy Queen!" Coronado's men had planted stakes in the ground to mark their passage, and they'd needed those stakes to be able to find their way back, for in all their trekking they'd found nothing of gold but the beating sun. The only city at the end of the trail was an Indian village. Mud huts . . . "And aren't we still trekking after those fabulous cities of gold?" was the windup. "Hollywood, Vegas, Silicon Valley, no different. Same old dream."

Yes, it had been quite a performance . . .

Weren't they in Missouri by now? Or still in Oklahoma? Sam's eyes shot open. Not a clue. The billboards were standard, they could be anywhere. PEPSI . . . GOLDEN PAWN . . . E-Z BAIL BOND . . . Car dealers and cigarettes. Vasectomy reversal. No walnut bowls or wood carvings, no caverns, so chances were this was not yet Missouri. Sam was no sleepier than before, and there was little point persisting in the pretense of sleep; his sham nap seemed to have done the trick of halting conversation before it came too close.

Sam's moods were so volatile, he almost laughed out loud. The driver seemed to be off in his own world now, busy and intent, pinkie delicately gouging his ear for wax, and Sam had just noticed that the man's right earlobe was lower than his left. That was his listening ear, and it looked to be stretched and sagging.

Too many sad tales . . . He'd probably heard them all, one time or another. "Is that right?" he'd say, or "Well, now . . . ," reserving judgment, keeping his true thoughts to himself.

All the houses they passed looked battened down for the night. Blacked out, mostly. Here and there, a television screen cast blue and shimmering light into the darkness. Aquarium light . . . And here was a scene: a window touched with gold. Framed within it, as though on a stage, two figures sat in cushioned chairs, both reading. They were not young. Stalled at a traffic light, Sam couldn't help staring at them, basking in the brightness, the borrowed warmth. "Creature comfort"—the phrase leapt to mind. They sat catty-corner from one another, the man and the woman, wrapped in a kind of blessedness, a halo of lamplight round each bowed head. Then, abruptly, as if she'd noticed Sam's prying gaze, the woman stood and whipped down the shade. *A cage,* Sam amended, *however gilded, it's still a cage, a golden cyst* . . . The driver raised four fingers to a passing truck; it was a semi, free of its trailer, only the cab speeding along, rattling its idle chains. Enough. Sam folded his glasses and pocketed them. Then he tipped back his chair and closed his eyes once more.

He wanted . . . What was it he wanted?

To be joined—to someone, or something, he wanted not to be bothered, there was nothing he wanted now. He wanted to want again.

Sure, he'd had his house dreams once—right down to the welcome mat at the front door and the barbecue grill out back, patio, rec room, and double garage in between. It was part of the having-your-own-family dream; he'd had all the usual dreams once upon a time. He'd been working as a chemist in those days, great-paying job, all the fringe benefits. He'd met Beverly, his wife-to-be, at the plant's pension office: she was a temp then but a powerhouse, high octane, that was clear right from the start.

Lately, looking back, it seemed clear to Sam that all his best time with Beverly revolved around the house. How had he failed to observe this? He must have noticed, but he'd put the best possible construction on it: she was a nester, and that was fine with him. He, too, wanted a nest. He couldn't recall when exactly they'd started spending their weekends going around to real estate offices and open houses together, but already he must have been onto her true interest for he waited to propose until they'd found what she wanted—a three-bedroom "storybook cottage" with white wood siding, blue trim, and a half-acre lawn with rambler roses draped over a white picket fence. They'd moved in after the wedding, then used their weekends and leisure time remodeling, planning the add-ons, scraping and borrowing, finagling payments. Beverly wanted gallery lights and recessed shelving in the living room, and he'd given her those things; he'd worn his knees to the bone tearing away the perfectly decent wall-to-wall carpeting that covered the living room, sanding and buffing the hardwood floor beneath it. And, in hindsight, wasn't that an irony, what with his being in carpet restoration now?

Beverly was always a lady; she never bitched or nagged, and the end came quietly, almost matter-of-factly. They sat across from one another at the dining room table; its fine mahogany was dustless, varnished to a high gloss. Sam recalled this minor detail so sharply because Beverly's nails were also glossy, varnished with clear polish—she never used color—and they tapped against the tabletop as she reviewed mortgage papers, patio estimates, bank records, turning the pages crisply, stacking and restacking them. For some reason, the gloss, the glaze, her light tapping with such heavy reverberations, as though carried by some dense medium, made Sam think of one of those glass paperweight spheres. There they were, a diminished Sam and Beverly—alive but captive in a glass bubble filled with water—a wedding-cake bride and groom, pinned forever sitting across from each other on matchstick chairs at a matchstick table, tiny flakes of confetti snow swirling upward from their feet at the least disturbance. And when Beverly spoke next, she might as well have shredded the papers between them, stirred the scraps and set them swirling, burying hands, shoulders, heads, the table itself. "We aren't going to make it" was what she said. When Sam suggested, "Let's see what we can work out till I'm back on my feet," she was perfectly cordial, reasonable, and firm. Her answer, Sam realized, covered their house and marriage in one. "Let's cut our losses now" was how he remembered it.

And what else was it she'd come up with? Oh, yes, this was the killer: "Credit is another name for confidence."

After it was all over, Sam had sworn never to become a homeowner again. It needed no vow. Talk about *confidence!* He was out of pep, drained of ambition. Renting was more his speed; this was realism, simple prudence. And look how much freer he was, dispensed from all concern for acquisition and repair! To be a renter was no disgrace—he had only to glance around him here to remind himself how much luckier he was than plenty of others. All the same, in his passage from owner to renter, Sam couldn't help feeling that he'd lost his purchase not only on the American dream but on life itself somehow.

As for Beverly, no hard feelings. She had a head on her shoulders and was using it, how could anyone blame her for that? It's what attracted Sam to her in the first place. Last he'd heard, nearly a year ago, she'd landed a government job at the Bureau of Standards in D.C. He'd forgotten exactly what G-level it was but knew it was big money; she was sure to be sitting pretty way up there.

ONCE STARTED, SAM AND I WERE ROLLING RIGHT ALONG, chatting about one thing or another, whatever came to mind. He was good company, out of the usual—I liked that. Our conversation lasted, I'd say, about seventy miles. Then all of a sudden—the door slammed. Silence. His eyes were shut but I could've sworn he wasn't sleeping. He had the look on his face of a man counting. Counting what? That I couldn't say— money, beans in a jar, anything—but definitely counting. Had to leave him be, though, leave him to it. From here on out, I was on my own.

Though—wait—not entirely, not yet. Scanning the passenger mirror for signs of life, I caught the gleam of eyewhite. The rest of the man was dark but not invisible. I could make out his legs— long ones—stretched clear across the aisle. Must've been well over six feet, I couldn't blame him for feeling cramped. Anything blocking the aisle was hazard, a clear violation, but I wasn't about to say a word—my usual cowardice with fellows of his size and racial persuasion. *And after all,* I told myself, *suppose I hadn't happened to glance his way at exactly that moment?* So I redirected my gaze elsewhere.

Nights, like I said, you're apt to hear the damndest things. Politics, personal gripes, deep thoughts, and just plain crazy ones; the later it got, the harder to tell one kind of talk from the other.

And, sooner or later, there was bound to be God talk, some fellow out to evangelize. It rarely worked.

"Somebody up in the sky taking notes? C'mon! Get real. Credits for good behavior? Look around! Just look around!" was the usual objection. The evangelist had an answer for this, too: "Praise the Lord anyway," he'd say.

In the quiet pauses, the sounds of nesting continued, the soft flurries of people bedding down, fussing with pillows if they had them, or making do with beach towels, bunched-up sweatshirts, or backpacks, whatever was handy. Needless to say, I envied them. I was facing a long file of double-tandem trucks up ahead. Double trouble, as far as I was concerned, though they were plenty visible, lit up like Christmas trees to let you know just how big they were. First real hill, I'd have to pass them. I didn't look forward to it, knowing how they'd speed up and do their damndest to overtake me on the downslope.

Night driving was my least favorite part of the job. It never got any easier. Most of the drivers felt the same way—we were all terrified of falling asleep at the wheel. Or of starting to see things that weren't there. What things? Night critters, for a start: hoot owls staring back at you from a dark wood, eyes of a fox flashing fire in the middle of the road.

Drive too long without resting and I'd start obsessing about roadkill—dog, cow, coyote, possum, deer, armadillo, skunk—all stages: fresh and humped, bloated or flattened, sawed or splattered. The red earth of Oklahoma, even in daylight, would begin to look bloody after miles of staring at it. There was road kill aplenty between Missouri and Oklahoma, less so west of Elk City, where what they liked to call used-cow dealers hauled dead cattle off to the rendering plant on a daily basis.

Drive long enough, late enough, and you're apt to see some fresh roadkill struggle to its feet and come straight at you, eyes flaring like headlamps. Worse yet—empty road, the times you feel you're floating down the freeway on autopilot, serene, not a care in the world. That's when accidents are bound to happen.

There's a dream I keep having, one of those nightmares I could live without. It's late night, or before dawn, and it happens in, oh, a bunch of ways, but it's one and the same dream. I'm driving an extra schedule, been driving for God knows how long, moving in and out of weather, speeding down the road. It's always an unlined road, but it isn't one-way. Everything I look at is shimmering, shaking, blurring. The few rigs on the road—stock trailers, oil trucks, auto haulers, cross-country movers—all look like hay wagons to me, that's how blurry. I'm picking up speed when the steering wheel comes off in my hands. Can't reach the foot brake, all I can do is—*useless!*—grab the wheel tight. Oil truck ahead. Right before slamming into him, I lurch into free fall, heart zooming, teeth zinging, already dead and wide awake . . .

The strange part is my not once thinking of the emergency brake. I'd have wrecked the engine block, sure, but consider the alternative. Another thing: I've never had this dream deadheading back from a run and, thank goodness, never *on* the job—only when I'm safely back home, snugged up in bed.

WHAT WAS THE DRIVER HARPING ON WHEN SAM TUNED HIM out? Oh, yes, Terre Haute, Indiana . . . picking up ex-prisoners as they're released from the pen in Terre Haute . . . "They give them a bus ticket, fifty dollars, and a new suit." The ex-cons tended to be politer than many of his other customers. "No way you'd ever know," he said, "except they happen to be carrying all they own in a paper bag. Real nice, same as you or me."

Nice didn't mean a thing to Sam. One of those purring, petting, cooing words was all. Besides, Sam had no illusions, he knew just how nice he was.

Sam still didn't feel the least bit drowsy. It made no difference; eyes open, shut, images kept him busy. Now the dimness, the enclosure, made him feel as though he were deep inside a tunnel. Someplace underground . . . the light soiled, brownish. He was standing, late at night, on a subway platform in lower Manhattan. Grand Street. That was on his last visit to the city, risking life and limb to save a few bucks in cab fare. The train hurtling past, an uptown express, seemed near empty. But the end car was occupied, full of faceless figures—men or women, he couldn't tell—with hats pulled down against the light, coat collars drawn up against the cold. They weren't going anywhere but back and forth the length of the borough from Bowery to Bronx, trying to catch a little sleep. Sam hadn't dreamed this, this special car, he'd seen it with waking eyes. Afterward, he was haunted by it; the whole rest of that visit he couldn't walk down a street without seeing shadow faces—cement and mud colored—lurking in the sewer gratings under his feet.

But that wasn't his problem, Sam had to remind himself. He wasn't homeless, wasn't destitute; he still had some prospects. His luck might yet take a turn. And surely he hadn't meant to be yakking on with the driver like one of those talk-show guests with yet another of those weepy confessions people never seemed to tire of.

AT SOME POINT IT ALWAYS GOT TO ME: JUST ABOUT everybody—my passengers, my wife at home—sleeping while I trudged on alone. I don't begrudge other folks normal sleeping hours even if I don't enjoy that luxury myself. Still . . . I'm human. Feel like I'm fighting gravity sometimes. I keep a thermos on the dash—even with all that caffeine, my eyes get stuck, banded to the yellow line, the line jotted, then steady, then jotted again. Sometimes my eyeballs seem to swell, so stretched with watching. It sure would help to have another driver along; he'd be deadheading home and closing his eyes now and then, but in between those times, together we'd talk up a storm, solve all the problems of the world.

I tried to think of my vacation coming up in September. It's Michigan this year, though the destination hardly matters to me. Vacation, for me, means wife at the wheel. That's the charm—leaning back, my hands and eyes idling for a change, letting the road stream by, stream through me, like water, erasing things as it goes . . .

All That Road GOING

Gradually, I realized that, while the heaters were working, the blowers were shot—almost no output. Only a matter of time before people started to notice. As a rule, I tried to keep the cabin cold, one of my little tricks for staying awake. I'd pretend the heating system was out of whack, then turn it up ever so slightly when the complaints grew to be a chorus.

And here came something. The spiky-haired gal with the chopped T-shirt, midriff bared. Bet she was freezing and whose fault might that be? Even though expecting her, I jumped a little when she tapped my shoulder, so soundless was her approach. She was standing right beside me before I noticed her bare feet.

Turned out, this wasn't about the cold. She pressed a wad of paper into my palm—a note—then turned on her heel without waiting for reply. I tracked her return in the passenger mirror. Once she'd resettled, I uncrumpled her note and read:

THAT MAN SCARES ME

All it said. I didn't have to ask which man. It had to be the fellow in the wool cap sitting across the aisle from her. I did wonder what his hands were up to; his head was sliced off by my mirror at chin level. Below that, I couldn't see a thing.

And then this crazy thought came to me, *Maybe that cap's the only roof over his head, maybe that's all it is . . .* However you looked at it, though, I was obliged to pull over at the next truck stop and check him out. Right then, any excuse for stopping sooner rather than later was fine by me, even if it did mean filling out a late arrival form at the end of my run. A ten-minute rest stop should do it, I figured.

The scary fellow would either step outside, leaving me free to scout around his seat for what I might find, or he'd remain inside and I'd be able to confront him face-to-face, without a crowd looking on. Not that I'd relish the opportunity for more conversation than we'd already had—I didn't expect it to be pleasant.

Next exit. I took it slow, a slow untwisting. It was strange . . . Strange things can happen at any time, but with double frequency, seems like, as night wore on. I found a place to park close by where one of the security officers was standing. Couldn't recall his name, but his face was familiar; we'd had dealings before. I hailed him, signaled him to wait.

When it became clear that everyone intending to get off the bus had done so, I counted the passengers remaining on board. There were six, the wool cap among them, and that lost little gal from Noplace, Missouri, who'd been so quiet I'd nearly forgotten her.

I told the officer I had a favor to ask. "Would you mind checking . . . ?" Would he mind hopping on board and taking a look—at the man at the back in the wool cap, in particular?

He obliged me by stepping inside and looking around. I kept my eye on him as he moved on through to the back of the bus, fiddling with an overhead light here, an armrest there. Back out, he shrugged, found little to report. "Just another bum sleazing through life," in his judgment. "I've seen worse. What's the problem?"

"Nothing. A feeling. He scares people."

"Feeling's not actionable. Ticket OK?"

"All correct," I had to admit. "So you think there's nothing to worry about?"

"Didn't say that. Far as I can tell, he's just a slob. Could use a bath. That's unpleasant, but it's not a crime. He seems to be well out of it, anyway. Sound asleep."

So. I was back to square one. All I had was a hunch, a gut feeling. Could have been way off base. I had to keep reminding myself how this was only the middle of the journey for most, all I was ever privy to. Couldn't stop whatever was going to happen from happening. If I knew what it was, I could try, but I couldn't read the future, I didn't know.

By the time I completed my headcount prior to starting up again, the man in the wool cap really did seem to be out of it. His eyes were closed, head bowed to his chest. The punky gal who'd handed me the note reboarded. She was wearing shoes now, I noticed, and a man's cotton shirt over a skimpy top; everybody else had piled on jackets and sweaters. Seemed like she'd dolled herself up a bit while she was at it: fresh doodads dangling from her ears, her hair—damped or gelled—spikier than before, and she'd drawn curlicues with a black pencil at the corners of her eyelids. Had that same little swag to her walk as she moved down the aisle. Then—came to a dead halt as she spotted the man who'd scared her still in the same place. She must have expected the police to haul him off at her convenience while she was prettying up in the powder room, because she froze halfway down the aisle. But the man in question, as she could see for herself, was fast asleep, and she moved on then, settling down quietly in her old seat. I was ready to go back there and find her a place elsewhere, if it came to that, but it turned out not to be necessary.

And, pretty soon, she too was snoozing, along with most everybody else. By then, I was hitting the thermos hard to keep awake. It was pretty darn lonesome up there in my captain's chair.

I envied the sleepers while knowing full well that one night's sleep couldn't begin to touch my tiredness. I'd seen too much over the years, too many nights, too many miles . . . Found a newborn once, fast asleep, in a bag somebody left on the seat, did I mention it? Mommy, or whoever parked it there, was long gone by the time we put a trace on the ticket. It was a gift bag, one of those glitter deals, silvery, you couldn't miss it. But better not get me started on *that* . . .

On Their Own

I'D BEEN THINKING ABOUT THAT BABY IN THE BAG, THEN
kids in general, how hard they had it nowadays, when there they
were: a mom and two little ones, waiting at the next flag stop.
Like I'd dreamed them into being, you know?

Couldn't say what it was, the hour, my eyes already spent,
or whatever they put in that special security bulb they use, that
turned the three of them so sallow toned.

Just my luck! The kids, brother and sister, were going to be
traveling on their own. Would I keep an eye out for them? How
old was the boy? Eight, but grown up for his age. The girl was six,
prettiest little thing once you got her out from under that light,
pure towhead.

I made sure someone would be on hand to meet them in
Philadelphia and promised to see to their transfer in St. Louis.

The boy wanted his skateboard with him. So, fine, OK by
me, but he'd have to find a place for it in one of the overhead
racks, I'd help him stow it; otherwise, it would have to go into
the freight compartment. His backpack would be no problem; he

could shove it under his seat. Finding—or arranging for—two seats side by side for the brother and sister together would take some doing, though. I kept the two of them waiting outside while I stepped back into the bus to take stock. I counted three empties in all. There was one close to the front that the girl from Hunters Junction had vacated, but the old lady settled there was liable to talk anyone's ear off. And besides, that would have meant separating the kids. There were two seats in back, not together, but close by. One was right opposite the toilet door, not the most pleasant. A young woman in a purple jogging suit had spread out to make it look like two people were already sitting there. (I know all the little schemes.) She was about a size and a half of what she should be; a kid would be the most comfortable riding companion she could hope for. The other empty was next to that grungy fellow in the wool cap. He was awake now, or at least his eyes were open. About time he cleared the seat beside him—the free ride was over.

So I moved on back there to give the two of them fair warning.

Not that I was eager for a fight—but I wasn't about to beat around the bush either. I put it to him, the man in the wool cap: anyone or anything occupying a seat had to have a ticket. I thumped the duffle so he couldn't miss what I was talking about: "This fellow here, where's his ticket?" You'd think that might get a laugh out of him, but he remained straight faced. Sat there playing deaf and dumb, not moving a muscle. Then I raised my voice loud enough to get through even if his ears were stuffed with cotton balls under his cap. "You're going to have to stow this somewhere. Under your seat or up in the overhead rack, I don't care which, but it's gotta go . . ."

Nothing in reply. Was he even breathing? Not a pulse, not a flicker to show there was anybody under that cap alive and listening. I was getting pretty pumped by then. I started to reach . . .

His hand shot out to forestall mine.

He surprised me, lifting the duffle with both hands and jamming it down under his feet; then, still clasping his lunch box, he slid over, close to the window, proving that he'd heard me, all right. At no time did he ever look me in the face, eye to eye.

It was not the best setup in the world, I was mindful of that, but it was the best I could arrange at the time. The boy would have an aisle seat and be able to keep an eye on his sister two rows behind him. I fully intended to keep my eye on both of them.

Then I summoned the kids on board and personally escorted them to the seats I'd cleared for them.

It was the boy who answered when I asked their names: "I'm Clem—she's Sasha." The girl must have been too bashful to speak for herself. I told them both—speaking through the boy, really—that they were to come up front and let me know if they ran into any problems.

CLEM WAS THE SMART ONE. HE COULD READ NEARLY ALL the signs: STOP, SLOW, SPEED . . . He couldn't read the one that started *yi*. Even though he knew the letters one by one, each and every one: YIELD, the letters all together made no sense to him. And yet he could put together some of the longer words, like WELCOME, and whole sentences, like GOOD BUY, CARTHAGE on the roof of a shopping mall as they left a town named Carthage.

Sasha was six but couldn't read any words, not one. She knew that stop signs and slow signs had different shapes and colors, though. She knew the numbers up to nine, but only sometimes. Her head was stuffed with pictures.

Clem knew he was clever—he knew words and numbers and shapes—that's why he was boss. That's why Sasha had to mind him.

His mom was a whole other story. Not too smart herself, but Clem couldn't tell her a thing. She was in trouble again, that's why they were being sent away, she couldn't fool him. She'd pulled herself together to get them tickets at least and made plans for who'd be meeting them in Philadelphia, and she'd gotten them

All That Road GOING

to the station in time—Clem had to hand her that. She'd even taken the trouble to think of treats, getting them hamburgers and fries and afterward letting them choose their own candy bars. He chose a Mars; Sasha picked out a Twix, not because she liked the taste—she didn't even know what it would be—but because it was wrapped in red paper and red was her favorite color. That's the way her thinking went, if you could call it thinking.

Clem still held his backpack on his lap, mindful that way down inside it, near the bottom, was the baggie with the money in it. Before they left, his mom had given him twenty dollars—a ten, a five, and five single dollar bills—more money than he'd ever had in his entire life. She'd remembered to give him a bunch of quarters as well, for phone calls. So Clem was all set. On his way to Aunt Penny's in Philadelphia, his first really big trip—near a thousand miles—and on his own.

He didn't bother to wave, though he was sure his mom would still be there, standing at the side of the bus until it pulled out. She wouldn't be able to see him anyways, since he didn't have a window seat. Besides, she'd said good-bye to both of them already with her slobbering kisses. She wasn't drunk yet, and she wasn't high on anything for a change. Last night she'd locked Kurt out of the house, but he'd spent the night parked on the curb in front. Clem had spied on him; he'd lifted the shade half an inch, enough to see and not be seen; he knew exactly what he was looking for. You had to squint hard to make out the shadow of the man, his knees peeking up over the window ledge. By tonight, Kurt would be back in their house, whooping it up and slapping his mom around—nothing Clem could do to stop it. Anyways, that very minute, Sasha started clambering up on her seat, trying to see out the back windows. Clem raised himself and ordered her to sit. When she paid no attention, he raised himself up and stepped on back there. "You set now!" he ordered and shoved her down. "You're suppose to mind me!" If the bus had started to move, she could of fallen backward and broken her neck, and Clem would be in for big trouble.

"I'm gonna give you such a smack . . ." If she tried any funny business again, he would. "You better mind me, or else! Gonna tell on you if you don't quit . . ." Clem searched Sasha's face to find out whether she was taking this in, but there was no way to tell—her eyes roamed clear past him. One thing about eyes: you could force a face or a whole body to turn around to where you wanted but not eyes, you couldn't force eyes.

Clem knew he was nothing much to look at, all skin and bones; his wrists and ankles poked out, he'd shot up so much in the last year. Sasha was smaller but had more meat on her. And more color. People took to her, not to him. Her hair was like corn silk, his—dull as hay in winter. Sasha knew how pretty she was; she was proud of her hair and carried a hairbrush with her everywhere she went.

At last they were starting to move! Clem did take a peek, only because he was curious, and his mom *was* standing there along-side the bus and, sure enough, she was waving to the wrong window. And she kept on standing there, her hand lifted, she kept it that way even after they were halfway down the street, when she must of known it was completely wasted.

Sasha, sitting finally, was busy with other things. She'd plunged deep into her Pocahontas bag and come up with her favorite doll. Not Barbie—Kim. She made the doll walk by swinging it from side to side. Suddenly, she shouted out, "We got fun?" Clem never-minded her, so she shouted again even louder, "Clem, I ast you—we got fun?"

"What do *you* think?" Clem said.

"I ast you," she repeated. "Ainit fun, Clem?"

"Ain't for me," Clem said.

Rummaging in his backpack, Clem touched base with the baggie with the money in it. *Safe and sound.* Then he fingered the white cardboard box his mom had made him promise not to open till Philadelphia after they were unpacked and settled in. It was meant to be a surprise. He would just peek. He pried open the side flap. Bubble wrap made fat whatever was hidden inside.

He yanked the mess, tugging the plastic covering left and right to free the thing, which turned out to be a silver-framed photo of the three of them, taken back in September. In the picture, Sasha and his mom's heads leaned together, their hair mixed together. Clem was on the other side, leaning away from the both of them, almost cut off by the frame. Across the glass, his mom had written in stiff gobs of Wite-Out, that gook she used to erase mistakes in typing I LOVE YOU. *Yeah, sure.*

If Sasha got wild, he might have to spoil the surprise and show her the photo before they got to Philadelphia. But, no—that would be stupid—it would only set her off, she'd start bawling. The bubble wrap would make her happy, though; she loved popping any kind of bubbles. With that in mind, he separated the wrap from the photograph and slipped the photo, loose and easy now, back into its box, then zipped up his backpack and shoved it down under his feet.

Just then the man sitting beside him burst out, "Don't robot me!" For a second, Clem thought the man was trying to say something to him, but he wasn't even looking at Clem, or at anyone. His voice was quieter when he spoke next: "Regrettably, we are forced to speak in the only way people can be counted on to listen." The sound coming out was as thin as an egg-whisk scraping. "People must be *made* to listen."

Clem sat face forward, staring at nothing, pretending he heard nothing.

"Sad, but true . . ." The man in the wool cap bent down to wrestle with the duffle between his feet; he came up with a clump of newspaper so tightly folded that it opened in pleats. His eye moved down and across the columns, scanning page after page exactly like a robot would, inch by inch as he moved down the columns. He halted at a police sketch of a man in a hooded sweatshirt, with a fringe of curly hair over his forehead. The eyes in the sketch were blacked out by sunglasses, but the face was hard to forget—long and pointy like a wolf. The man in the wool cap stared at the face in the newspaper and smiled to himself. His own face, with nose so short and cheeks so wide, couldn't be more different. Clem stretched his neck a little to find out what the police sketch was for, but was only able to make out the first letters, *Sus*—and, maybe, was it?—*B?* . . . No, it was *P.*

Susp. What kind of word was that?

A sharp crackle; the newspaper was folded up.

When the man reached down into his duffle a second time, he came up with a headset. But only the earphones, the center wire dangling free. Then his fingers fussed under his cap, fitting his ears with the little round receiver buttons, and his head began nodding like there really was a tape player attached and something he wanted to hear really playing on it. Clem was alert to every move the man made—it was all so wild and weird!—but he did his best not to stare.

"That's a lie," the man said loudly. "Name it, laminate it—it's still a lie. Bad gossip."

He went on, voice calm: "See, no." He nodded, then froze. "What's wrong with his attitude?" Now he was acting like he had a cell phone, making believe he was listening to somebody talking to him, trying to sound important like he was the boss. "Product placement is the key," he said, "preempt them! Hear what I said? P-p-p-pre-empty product placement!" Spit glistened in the corner of his lip. When he started blurting out "Netgeer! Samsung! Yepp! Yeti! Getty! Game Boy! Creation Station," Clem recognized some of the names, but some he could only guess at.

Weeeeird! Clem was tempted to give an ear-winding signal to somebody, anybody, even his dum-dum sister, he needed to let somebody know what a screwball this guy was, and that he—Clem—wasn't the one making the racket. But nobody minded. Nobody seemed to notice. Clem decided to switch on the reading light overhead; the dark was making everything more spooky than it should be. He took care to angle the light to cover only his own seat, though, so as not to get the man more riled than he already was. All Clem wanted was to feel safe in his own seat. The man was almost whispering now; Clem heard him say, "Nickels and dimes, nickels and dimes—stay out of it." More mumble-jumble, it was all just a kind of drooling, Clem decided, and a waste of time trying to make sense of it. Clem was still hoping to start up a conversation with somebody intelligent and not crazy, but that didn't look like it was going to happen anytime soon. The man beside him went on, sometimes loud and bickering, sometimes soft, the voice speaking to itself, speaking to no one: "That's none of your concern," spacing each word. "Too bad, but it's back to the quiet room with him." Hard to listen to much more of this, and Clem couldn't help interrupting with the first thing that popped into his head: "Could you tell me what time it is?"

"So I'm saying . . . ," the man continued without a pause, "go in there and consolidate." Clem asked again, and this time the man glared back at him, waving his bare wrist in Clem's face by way of reply.

It was weird, all right. He was right beside Clem and, at the same time, far, far away in his head somewhere, lost in some other world.

Clem got a good look at how grungy the man was. The smell of him up close was even worse. Clem could care less about knowing the time, but he was going crazy for some real talk—not little girl talk, not retard talk. The man beside him was a real freak, no question. Interesting, though, in a way . . .

Then Sasha piped up. Same old song: "We got fun, Clem?"

Before Clem could make up his mind whether to answer her, the man beside him cried out in a small shivery voice: "That does it—we'll *sue!*"

Stories

THERE WAS A FRESH SPURT OF TALK AFTER WE STOPPED
to pick up the kids. It would taper off soon enough once we
hit the highway and, when that happened, I'd miss it. From
there on out, it would be pretty much me, myself, and my wheel
for company . . .

"We're in central time now, I bet," someone piped up, "same as
St. Louis." The voice was familiar, though it took me a moment to
place it. "Is Tucson Rocky Mountain or Pacific Coast time? I get
them all mixed up. What did I miss in Tucson, I wonder?"

It was the wedding—"year ago to the day"—I recognized.
Must've been a pair of new ears she'd found, for she was onto the
story of their nickname "R & R" for Robert and Roberta, how
much in love they were, how she'd been wrong—hadn't she been
wrong?—ever to doubt it . . .

"Tone it down, will you?" someone hollered from the row
behind her. And then directed at me: "Can't you stop them from
twittering? Won't somebody throw some towels over their cages
so they quit twittering and go to sleep . . ."

That was the go-ahead. The griping hour had arrived. Complaints were hollered from the back of the bus, were walked up, whispered privately in my ear. Back of the bus was too cold when the front was nice and toasty. When it got comfortable in back, it was broiling up front. I made a show of fiddling with the dials, faking it; there was no way to adjust the heating to satisfy each and every customer.

"STRANGE THING . . . YEAR BEFORE MY EYE TROUBLE GOT bad, had me a dream, dreamed I'd left my eyes in the cup where I usually keep my dentures, side of my bed . . ."

Pierson's new seatmate was a man, none too young, who'd been told he was going blind. It hadn't developed to the full extent yet, but he'd been assured by two specialists that it was bound to come. He'd have to start practicing with a cane and learning Braille when he got back to New York. Pierson wasn't convinced of any of the man's story. For one thing, he didn't *act* blind. And his eyes were not as clouded as you'd expect. To hear tell, he'd been everywhere, done everything—Pierson didn't believe that either. He called himself a philosopher, was full of wise saws—a motto a mile, it seemed: "Sweat never drowned anyone," and "A man looking for easy work is sure to go to bed tired," and "You can be anything you want to be. Where there's a will . . ."

Pierson couldn't have wangled a word in edgewise had he wanted to. Why did he always get stuck with people like this? Or was it his own silence that called it forth? The man's mouth opened and shut, sounds dribbled out, but he wasn't even listening to himself. Twice, he halted in midsentence to ask: "Now what was I saying?"

The man had flown out one way—and was making a slow journey back by bus. He still called Vinita, Oklahoma, home—it was where he'd started from when he ran away as a boy of eleven. Hard to believe that was over sixty years ago and that, with all his other comings and goings, he'd never even tried to go back in all those years. Of course, the town looked pretty small and shabby to him now, he could tell that much, even with his eyesight near gone. Small and shabby—and innocent. Untouched by time in some ways but in others completely changed. By now, all his kinfolk in Vinita were either dead or couldn't recall who he was; he'd had to stay at a motel. His grandpa had warned him of what would happen if he broke the ties, and it turned out exactly as the old man had foretold. But he'd been young, too hepped up and full of himself to listen to anybody else in those bygone days.

After he'd left Vinita, he landed in Chicago. Fancy hotel, torn down since. There he'd worked as a bellhop and learned more than he ever wanted to know about life—the seamy side anyhow. Then—there were a bunch of jobs after that—he'd somehow gotten into off-track betting. That had taken him to New York—uptown Manhattan, and he'd stayed on there long enough to buy a share in the nightclub where he'd been tending bar. It was called the Hot Spot, a jazz hangout, and was quite something in its day. A black man owned it, he'd been working for a black man. "Can you believe that?" he asked Pierson. "My boss was a black man!"

"I'm not prejudiced against blacks," he was quick to add. "Thing is, though, you can't ever know them well enough to trust them, you never know what they're thinking. Can't even tell their age."

He'd made a heap of money in his time. Only reason he was going by bus now was to take in slowly all that he'd missed noticing the first time around. He'd boarded a bus out of Vinita to St. Louis back then and hitched the rest of the way, arriving in Chicago with three dollars in his pocket.

Funny, his going back only when his sight was near gone . . . He wondered sometimes: What if he'd lasted it out in Vinita? What would he be doing now? Pumping gas? Making curly fries? Would he even recognize himself if he passed himself on the street? And would he have been happier, after all?

"You don't know the half of it . . . ," the man went on.

All these little confessions were getting to Pierson. The trucker who'd been sitting beside him before had been bad enough, but this man was worse. Now he was back onto the subject of wives. He'd wanted a wife, wanted kids, to take care of him in his old age, but never could stick around long enough to start a family. "Wish I had my life to do over," he sighed. "I guarantee you some major changes. Back then, I couldn't ever imagine myself getting old. I never dreamed . . ."

The man kept at it while Pierson's mind wandered. How had he come to count on Marie? He *had* counted on her, much as he hated to admit it, depending on her more and more as the years wore on. Got to taking it for granted that she'd always be there for him. And wasn't that what he'd been thinking, deep down, despite his better judgment, when they'd met at Swanson's Café? They'd never been in love, never a word from him to suggest any such thing. And never a contract to tie them up in knots. She was waitressing when they met; he'd come in for coffee and pie. Treated him special right from the start, making sure that even his second cup was fresh brewed, cutting an extra-generous wedge of pie for him, with all the filling left over from the earlier cuts spooned over onto his plate. Always a special touch. And then when Pierson was out of work and as down in the dumps as ever he'd been, she'd out-and-out proposed to him: "Why not come home with me. I'll look after you."

Marie was in good health then, better shape than he was, what with his smoking three packs a day, late nights at bars, and fast food for meals when he thought of meals at all—most of the time, he couldn't be bothered. She got him to quit his smoking and boozing, packed him with protein. He'd been a scarecrow when they met and, in a matter of months, she had him feeling bouncier and looking better than he had in years. Marie was plump, a plain Jane, but solid, humming with energy in those days, and she'd taken care of him exactly as she'd promised. They lived in half of the duplex she inherited from her mother, rented the other half. The house would go to her niece after this. Every year, soon as things warmed up, she'd reserved the lakeside cabin in Colorado. He liked to fish—really, he liked to be out of doors and doing nothing with nobody hassling him. Catching anything wasn't the point. He could spend whole days dangling a string in the water, it rested him.

Never grow old . . .

She'd given Pierson her word and he'd trusted it. Only in the last few weeks, when she couldn't pretend anymore, had he learned the dirty secret she'd been keeping for so long. For at least a year, she'd known she wouldn't be seeing him through, her promise wouldn't be kept. Pierson couldn't get over it—a whole year of lying to him!

Even so . . . He could still turn around and get back in time for her . . . go anywhere the hell he wanted on the one ticket. That's what a See America pass was for . . .

Get back, and do what? Get back, and say what? How could he ever explain himself? And, anyway, he couldn't move a muscle— that was the long and short of it, that's what kept him sitting here, hostage to whoever happened to land in the seat beside him.

THE VOICES WERE DIMMING NOW. A FEW SCATTERED SPARKS of conversation, none connecting, drifted my way. Then something soft, thick, a repeated "Ay, chulita . . . Ay, chulita . . ." Couldn't say what it meant, but I knew there was no harm in it. There were faint but toxic, tinny sounds from somebody's Walkman that set my teeth on edge. Be grateful it's not gangsta rap, I told myself, deciding not to notice unless it got louder, as long as no one was complaining.

We continued over forty miles in this way. When the Walkman faded away, I was almost grateful to hear Roberta pipe up. Same theme song but with something new added about how they'd first met, how it looked like pure coincidence but she knew it must have been fated, there was no other good explanation. She'd done sporting goods and domestics, she'd done cashier, and that very day she was supposed to be starting layaway, but they needed help in customer service. And that just so happened to be the very day that Robert happened to walk in. If that wasn't fate she didn't know what was. And right away, on the instant, she knew he was the one. "The one for ever and ever," she said, "I just *knew*."

"There's no such thing as forever," her companion said. "There never was."

I'd heard this sort of thing before, different words maybe, different voices, but the same mix—advice, complaint, confession. Hundreds of life stories that boiled down to six or seven. Or maybe three or four . . . If one was laid off, another was going to a new job; if one was on his last legs, another was about to give birth . . . Somebody running away from home, another—coming home after years, half a lifetime sometimes, of being gone. Sometimes, it was a spiritual home they'd be bound for—Graceland, Nashville, wherever . . . They'd be caught for a while in the one capsule, gathered, housed for the duration, then—scattered. I'd get to eavesdrop on their stories, but only the middles of them, never knowing how they turned out afterward. I couldn't even begin to guess how the big story—the one in which all the little stories fitted—might go.

Problem was I still believed in the big story—that there was one, a story that you and I and the other fellow were a part of, and that, if only I knew enough, the story would make sense—even when all the evidence seemed to be pointing the other way. I'm not a bit religious, that's the wife's department; if you catch me in church, it's only to keep her company—and for the singing, I like to sing.

The point was, I couldn't—still can't—stand thinking that all this going and coming didn't add up, someway.

But—bits and pieces, that's all I was dealt. Sometimes, having so little time and a merely mortal patience, I wanted to give those pieces a good shake to make them fit. Late times, in the small hours, like these . . .

Late Night

SLEEP WAS LIKE ANOTHER HOUSE. ALL DEE ANNA HAD TO do was to step through that open door. But she held back. She kept thinking of another stepping forward after years of holding back—that long-ago Sunday when she was sure she'd been saved. Her real mom was alive then, though already she looked like a scarecrow and had lost all her hair, even her eyebrows and eyelashes, and Dee Anna wondered now if she hadn't convinced herself that something real had happened only because she knew how much her mom had wanted it.

They would drive most Sundays over to Second Baptist Church in Stanton, and it was there Dee Anna had answered the altar call. The aisle sloped down to the mourners' bench and, right above it, to the black gleams of Brother Ray's shoes flashing and stomping. The choir was singing, "He's all right!" Dee Anna could still see that long, narrow stretch of rug. Looked like it was drenched in blood. She couldn't feel her feet touch the carpet, but she could see that she was moving, riding that bloody arrow down, her arms reached out, her head and shoulders pitched forward. Jesus was leading, holding both her hands, folding them into his own, pressing them tight—a secret handshake to give her courage. His palms were warm and grainy, like unsanded wood. Ahead of them, down by the mourners' bench, somebody was playing the kazoo, that braying, blurty sound, and somebody was babbling in tongues—a whole bunch of somebodies babbling—and none of that mattered really because Jesus was smiling, yes, smiling, he had the sweetest . . . Then—sudden as he'd come to her, he vanished, cleared off like mist, and all Dee Anna could see was the mourners' bench, the lumpy figures huddled there; everything blurred, dissolving, her eyes so scalded with tears. She'd been baptized after that—gone under and come up spluttering—and had felt different for the whole rest of the week. But later, at her stepmom's church, they'd taught her that water baptism wasn't enough; you had to have the baptism of the Holy Ghost as well, and the only proof you had it was speaking in tongues. And you couldn't want or wish for it, you couldn't pray it down, it had to just come. But Dee Anna never did get the baptism of the Holy Ghost, never spoke in tongues of fire, not even once. She hadn't been saved, after all . . .

Dee Anna, fighting sleep now, kept swaying, catching her head as it looped to the side, lurching with each turn of the wheel. The driver must of been making up time. Dee Anna's neck was wrenched—her head aching in sympathy with her neck. She tried her best to lean away from the man sitting next to her; that way if her head started to swing, it would be into the aisle and would avoid brushing his shoulder. Not that he'd notice—he seemed to be well out of it, snoring softly and regularly, a low, mumbling whistle, sounding a little like ocean surf. Dee Anna had only visited the ocean once but never would forget the sound of it, the soft crash of the wave coming in, the seethe and hiss of the undertow.

Passing one of the few windows still lit at this hour, her eyes feasted. *Home* . . . a lamplit sitting room, the scene so sunny and sweet it might have been glazed in honey. *It's only a picture,* she had to tell herself, *lamps, chairs, people painted on glass.* And all of it, in an instant, swallowed up in darkness. *None of it real.* Yet how it glowed and beckoned to her . . .

Somewhere along in the wee hours, Dee Anna—she couldn't help it—finally let go. She closed her eyes and the other light switched on. It was bright, much too bright, and there was something in the air, this searing chill, it prickled her nose. Mr. Blue was there, already working; the sheet tented over her bent knees was a raised car hood and Mr. Blue was hunkered down, angling a trouble light under it. He kept checking, but when the baby crowned and Dee Anna cried out he was busy in another corner of the room twirling round and round on his piano stool. Now he was standing alongside her pressing her face into a blue pillow blue was all she saw she couldn't breathe . . . But the pillow flopped onto the floor and there it was, what he didn't want her to see: her baby born with a terrible stalk. Mr. Blue used a knife then his teeth then a handsaw it couldn't be cut couldn't be hidden it was a tree—short branches and no leaves. Look again, and full of leaves small and mitten shaped. Mr. Blue lifted the baby and the tree came with it leaves brushed Dee Anna's breasts . . . She cried out, her own cry woke her. Someone had touched her breasts, grazing like a leaf, lightly, the lightest of touches, yet piercing . . .

Wide awake, Dee Anna wasn't sure. Her breasts had tightened, though. The man beside her was drowsing, or faking it. One thing was clear: she had to keep herself from falling off again. She folded her arms tightly across her chest. And felt what she'd been dreading all along, the chill sparks, the dampness of her milk coming in.

EVERYBODY SLEEPING BUT ME . . . A COKE CAN WAS scuttling back and forth under the seats and into the aisle, leaving a sticky residue in its wake and making me half crazy. No one owned it, of course, no one wanted to take the responsibility. So what else was new? I'd been driving too long—I was starting to obsess again. Right then, my mind was onto residues—the wads of chewing gum under seats and armrests; when I tried to get off that subject, my mind turned to—same difference!—tire shreds from old blowouts roughing up the smooth stretches of highway. I badly needed to unkink. Duffy was up the road; it had a decent-enough snack bar and restrooms and such. I decided to call it a rest stop, even though there wasn't any stop scheduled at this hour, and never mind that everyone but yours truly was already resting.

Or that the usual exit ramp was barricaded with barrels. I'd have to go on past the ramp, take the next exit, and double back to the station. Just what I needed.

By the time we'd made it to the depot, I was in no mood for trifling. There were the expected groans of protest when I switched on the overhead lights. I'd interrupted their beauty naps—too bad! There'd be equal and opposite protest, I was willing to bet, when the call to reboard went out and I had to round them up again.

My announcement was one of the standard don't-hassle-me-or-you'll-regret-it varieties. Fair warning: "I'm not just flapping my lips here." I meant every word of it. "In case you don't believe in the hereafter—if you're not back on this bus by 2:45 A.M., you'll be here after. At least four hours, if I'm not mistaken."

After the passengers cleared out, I made my way down the aisle. The floor was filthy, scummy with trampled food, pop cans still oozing. Torn candy wraps. The tattered rags of a newspaper—looked like it'd been kicked down the line. I shouldn't dignify it by calling it a newspaper. Scandal sheet was the name for it in the old days—those were my days, too. This one was crammed with the usual—celeb tell-alls, tips on beating the lottery, pyramid schemes, the latest miracle diets and cures. Neat color shot of a cockatoo who'd dialed a rotary phone, called the fire department, and saved the building.

There was a special feature on what the astrological charts had to say about the relation of Mars to Venus and the importance of their conjunction for stock market decisions, romance, and games of chance. The reason why the stars should always be consulted; the line caught my eye: "We are covered with stardust, after all."

Stardust, my foot! What I saw was grime. Why did I bother with such trash? I crumpled up what remained of the paper, rescued a dropped shawl and flung it overhead, leaving the really nasty stuff for the mop-up crew.

INSIDE THE TERMINAL, DEE ANNA HEADED STRAIGHT FOR the ladies' room. The place was none too clean. Writing speckled the walls, four-letter words everywhere. On the door of the stall she chose, the words connected; they went back and forth, like a conversation. One person asking:

DON'T YOU JUST
LOVE SMALL ONES?

With another answering:

YES! BIG ONES ARE BRUTE-ALL

Over to the right, someone else had offered her two cents' worth:

NO—BUT I LIKE THEM JUST A LITTLE
IT AIN'T THE MEAT
IT'S THE MOTION!

And in a squeezed backhand under this, what appeared to be a fourth had joined in:

IS IT EITHER?

Dee Anna had no opinion, none, on any of this. But it was getting to her, everything getting to her now. She had to move—decide!—*do* something.

PIERSON FOUND HIMSELF VEERING TOWARD THE BANK of telephones as he paced. Veering and pulling away—correcting himself. One phone kept on squalling. The caller at this end probably failed to pay up, yet Pierson couldn't dismiss the feeling that the call was meant for him—he was being summoned. The idea was cockeyed, he'd be the first to admit it. How could he be reached by anyone else when he himself hadn't the foggiest idea where he was now? But the ringing never seemed to stop, and before Pierson knew what he was doing, he'd shot over to it and was pressing the receiver to his ear.

"Sweetie, I'm on my way." The voice was sugary—a woman speaking.

"Wrong number!" Pierson spat out, slamming the earpiece down with such clumsy force that it missed the hook. He had to hang up twice. The ringing resumed.

Turn back . . . He stood there staring at the earpiece, its snaking cord, without a thought in his head, his feet, as if under a spell, nailed to the ground. No saying how long this lasted. Seconds? Minutes? Too long. Then he shook his head and—it was weird— at that instant, the phone quit ringing. Pierson was free to move again. Felt like he was deciding for a second time and it was the same choice: no way he was going back to her.

Ducking into the door of the men's room, he nearly collided with someone just leaving. The man was in such a hurry that all Pierson could catch was the unwashed stench of him and the fact that he was wearing a winter cap pulled down to his eyebrows.

THE MAN IN THE WINTER CAP HEADED FOR THE SNACK bar. Lingered at the counter there, reading over the menu a couple of times. Chili or soup? Hot dog or corn dog or burrito? Jell-O or coffee or milk or soda or fruit juice? But then, abruptly, he turned away, ordering nothing.

Seated at a far table, waiting for his soup to cool, Sam Shevra observed the man without interest. The bowl was Styrofoam, a good insulator. Too good—it was taking forever. He was surprised to see the man in the knit cap bearing down on him, mouthing something unintelligible, and shocked when, without warning, the man came right up to him and stabbed his fingers directly into the bowl, prancing, trotting—strutting them!—through the steaming broth.

Not a word was said.

Sam pushed away from the table at once; his chair squawking. Only when he'd walked off a safe distance to a more populated spot did he dare turn back and regard the scene he'd fled.

The man in the cap was simply standing there, blowing on his fingers, which must have stung badly. A brief pause—and he settled himself into Sam's chair, the chair already warmed for him. His face remained impassive, with only a narrowing gaze as he dipped the spoon and raised it to his lips, then shook salt, shook pepper into the bowl. Yet Sam was sure the soup was still too hot to taste.

Did none of the other diners see? *How could they not see?* The others stooped over their plates and cups; nobody, but nobody, glanced up.

Did it really happen? Sam himself found it hard to believe. He'd ordered a bowl of soup and brought it to the table and now another man was sitting at that table and eating it. Was it really the same table, the same bowl of soup? Or was he—Sam—bone weary, half-asleep, dreaming with eyes open? But no—he recalled with perfect clarity the man's long fingernails, black rimmed; he hadn't made that up.

Sam felt himself actually shaking. *Shaking!* Anything could blow up at this hour, anything from the man in the knit cap at any hour . . . Shouldn't he report the incident? But what could Sam say if he tried? *A man walked through my soup?* "Huh? Run that by us again? Your soup, you say? Anybody else see this?" Sam himself would be marched off for observation.

Next time, no question—assuming he wasn't bankrupt—Sam promised himself he'd fly. Sure, it would cost, but the extra expense would be worth it. There were far too many creeps around.

He could have flown this time if he hadn't wasted two hundred bucks trying to beat the odds in Laughlin. Never done anything like that before—whatever possessed him? And now . . . going to pieces over a bowl of soup!

Sam tried to reason with himself, he believed in reason. *Simmer down! Keep that lid on . . .* It wasn't the loss of his snack that bothered him. No—soup wasn't the issue. Sam hadn't been that hungry to start with; he'd chosen to sit down with a bowl of soup to keep himself occupied, a way of passing time. It wasn't as if he had nothing to eat. As always when traveling, he'd brought some packets of dry oatmeal along. They were available at the moment if he really wanted—he'd left them in his carry-on bag and the bus was on the premises—but Sam decided to wait. At the next stop, if he felt the least bit hungry, he'd buy a cup of tea for the sake of the hot water and pocket the tea bag. He'd stir in the dry oats, then the sugar and cream to which he'd be entitled, and have himself some cheap, nourishing grub. He happened to like oatmeal, the taste and the way it filled him, even the look of it, its brainy texture.

Walk away . . .

It was a good thing, Sam reminded himself, that these past few years had taught him how little anyone really needed to get by. Needed, not wanted; wants were another story. The man in the watch cap was now standing—he'd already polished off the soup—and with expert swiftness was loading his pockets with saltines and small paper squares of sugar. Stuffing his pockets! So what was his lunch box for? It must have been light—conceivably empty—Sam could tell from the way he carried the thing. Why carry it if there was nothing in it? You had to wonder.

HAND AND HAND, CLEM AND SASHA MADE THEIR WAY through the waiting room. Sasha's steps were dragging to start, but they perked right up soon as she spotted the gift machine with all its goodies spread out on a spinning tray. There was a plastic dome over the tray, smudged with handprints; Clem and Sasha both peered intently through its murky lens. It was like a grab bag, Clem thought, the only difference being you could see everything beforehand. Sasha wanted the teeny baby doll inside her bottle. *How dumb can you get?* Clem marveled. *A baby inside its own bottle!* But Clem himself couldn't help being tempted; he'd spied a neat little set of three-inch, black metal throwing knives resting on a black leather carrying pouch—a real prize. He knew the machine was a gyp—what he'd end up with would be a keychain or a plastic whistle, or nothing at all if he let himself get sucked into it, so he yanked at Sasha; they had to get away for both their sakes.

Sasha kept whining and dragging as Clem tried to lead her away. Next, it was the snack bar and the Coke machine. Then she tugged at Clem's hand, trying to steer him over to the wall of flashing video games, but Clem's pull in the direction he wanted to go was stronger. They were on their way to the toilets at the other end of the waiting area, Clem was determined. He meant to arrive in Philadelphia with his twenty dollars untouched. He'd be needing it, he figured; sooner or later he planned to strike out on his own. He'd dump Sasha with their aunt, stock up on meals and whatever other freebies were around for the taking, and then, when he felt good and ready, when he'd gotten the lay of the land, take off.

Sasha was sulking when Clem ordered her to go to the toilet and take care of her business. So he gave her a light smack, back of her ear. That set her to whimpering and more stalling, until a lady happening by came to their rescue and offered to take her on inside. And Sasha followed along nicely, holding tight to the woman's hand.

Sasha did a whole lot better with strangers, Clem noticed, because it took a while for strangers to catch on to what was wrong with her. Clem watched the two of them disappear before he entered the men's room.

He was soaping his hands and face at the sink when somebody tapped him on the shoulder. Clem was so startled that his muscles gave a little jump. The tapper was a grown man; he had a bleached buzz cut in front and a long skinny rattail down his back. He was wearing a nifty Bulls jacket.

All That Road GOING

"That's a cute little gal I seen you with," he said.

"Yeah? So?"

"So—I give you fifty bucks for her."

"What?" The tile wall was too glossy—there was a glare.

"You wanna *buy* her? You shitting me? I can't sell my own sister!"

"Who's stopping you? Give you sixty . . ."

This couldn't be for real, Clem thought. Sasha was pure nuisance—what use could she be to anyone? But it was true, like the man said: there was nobody stopping him. His mom—Aunt Penny—they were both far away. He had no idea where his dad might be. There was nobody telling him what to do. "A hundred," Clem tossed back, playing along. It was some kind of game, wasn't it? Had to be. So why did he feel that even a hundred bucks was way too little?

The man in the Bulls jacket agreed to sixty-five, not a dime over. He said it was damn near all he had, allowing for carfare home and a couple beers on the way.

But now it looked like the man, slipping a wad of bills from an inside pocket, had gotten serious. The bills were folded in a silver clasp with a big blue stone on it. Clem couldn't remember the name of the stone, that greenish blue, tip of his tongue, but anyways. There was so much he wanted and meant to have, so many things he was saving up for. Most of all, he wanted Rollerblades, the racing kind they called rocket blades; after that, he wanted a Bandit trick bike, the one you could make stand up on its front or rear tires; and then he wanted a scooter, and a walkie-talkie, Nike Air shoes, and he wanted to get a Nike swoosh tattooed across his back. Once he got free of Sasha, he could do anything he wanted. In silence, Clem watched the man's hand, slapping the tens down on the sink rim. Six slaps; then Clem shook his head and said, "Sixty-five, and your Bulls jacket you're wearing, and it's a deal." Clem was echoing "it's a deal" from something he'd heard on TV. It was only a game.

"No fucking way, man. This jacket ain't for sale."

"Then I ain't selling nothing, neither."

With that, the man vanished, quick as a cat.

But he'd been real, Clem couldn't of made him up. He left Clem standing at the sink, faucet running, fingers draped under the pelting water, eyes wide, staring at the wall. It was like a secret window had opened and shut. Now he knew. Like that time they'd put a drop of tap water under the microscope in science class and seen for the first time what really went on there—all those silvery ghost fish swimming by, wagging and thrashing and biting. Gobbling each other whole.

You Are Here

WHEN SAM NEXT SPOTTED THE FRIGHTENED GIRL IN THE
old-lady dress she was reading posters, dawdling over each one,
although they couldn't have been that interesting. Earlier, when
he'd held the waiting room door open for her, she'd skittered by,
shrinking past him, without a word or a nod by way of thanks.
Her every gesture telegraphed distress. *It can't be that bad,* he
thought—but maybe it was.

Sam didn't know much about fashion, only enough to recognize that the girl was very young, that her dress was much too big
and the style decades old, as if she'd stepped out of some space-
time warp. She seemed to cry out for rescue, and Sam thought she
might be rushing to a telephone, but when he'd passed the bank of
phones she was nowhere in sight. Only one of the phones was in
use. A gray-haired man in tasseled loafers stood, receiver in hand,
facing away from the stall.

He was trying to explain something. "But, see," he said, and
his voice thickened, "time is no longer on my side . . ."

Sam moved quickly past, hands stuffed deep in his pockets, coins rattling. He was too upset to start over, find another table, and sit back down. And by now he'd lost what little appetite he'd had. He was still jarred from the soup incident—no longer shaking so it showed, although he felt it, his muscles tensed whenever he thought about it. Was this what people meant when they said so-and-so's nerves were high strung? But he'd been provoked.

More than ever at loose ends, Sam could not rest. He'd dry shaved during their last stop, not that many hours ago, so there was nothing he had to do now. He paced, reminding himself that he'd be sitting for hours yet. Besides, the chairs in the waiting area were the plastic bucket kind, none too welcoming. And suppose he did happen to fall asleep, only to be jolted awake at the boarding call, which couldn't be far off? Most of the people in those chairs sat slumped, eyes glazed or shut. A bearded young man sat blissed out, full lotus, amid the litter, on the unswept floor. It all looked strange.

Slowly but surely, the years since his layoff had turned even the familiar strange . . . simple things like mowing the lawn, stringing up Christmas lights, making out grocery lists, guest lists. Had he really done those things? He had. Once upon a time. Had the wife, the house; planned a family, almost made it. Two kids when they were set, boy and girl. Puppy to tag along with the kids, all that.

Almost—the story of his life.

Sam hadn't yet learned to let the sick tooth die; instead, he nudged the pain along, working his tongue over it, mouthing the words that hurt the most.

To a stranger listening in, the words escaping Sam, echoing something someone said to him about job skills, made no sense at all, sounded like "chopsticks." Sam often talked to himself, assuming he was unobserved or feeling too tired to care. It was the same-old, same-old wheel of words going round, "We'll let you know . . . We'll get back to you . . ." He was only venting; there was no progress of thought involved.

Someone was awake now—furiously awake, attacking a vending machine over in the corner. *Bet that hurt* . . . Sam registered the frenzied whump-whump-tlunk of a fist pounding metal—the place was a zoo! He didn't care to turn his head and assess the situation further. There was sure to be a number to call in case of malfunction posted above the return-change lever or button or whatever. In case the man cared to read. Apparently not, though . . . Now you could hear throttling noises, the machine being shaken, followed by two swift kicks. *It's this godforsaken hour,* Sam thought, *people who can't sleep coming unhinged. Better keep moving* . . .

PACING, DEE ANNA KEPT CLOSE TO THE TRAVELERS' AID office to start. The door to the office was shut tight, whoever worked there must have gone home hours before. Her heart was still hammering; she imagined people passing could hear it, so loud it was.

Trying to look occupied, she studied the posters on the wall. The one of a skinny dog—a greyhound, she supposed, she'd never seen one—was something left over from Christmas. In spite of his costume, a bright red Santa cap with a cotton-ball pom-pom and a green harness with jingle bells, he looked pinched and sad.

She recognized the scene of the Gateway Arch, but only from pictures. Next to it was an ad for San Francisco, saying WAY TO GO! showing a shiny new bus tilted up a hill. Below, arced a great bridge. The sky was lilac and gold. Someday Dee Anna hoped to see that bridge, that sky, with her own eyes. Would she ever?

Not far off was a bulletin board crammed with scraps of paper, what Sweet Satisfaction called a "wish-want-worry list." Studying it, as if she knew what she was looking for, would give her an excuse for just standing there.

One of the notices caught her eye right away:

FREE CASH!

COLLEGE. SCHOLARSHIPS. BUSINESS.

MEDICAL BILLS.

And in bold letters underneath:

NEVER REPAY!

Who did they expect to believe that "never repay"? In truth, you paid and paid, with interest added on. Who could be so dumb to think there was any other way? The address was for Miracle Loans, in Columbus, Ohio; there was a toll-free number.

What to do? . . . Time was she would have prayed over it, or at least gone through the motions, hoping there might be somebody up there who'd be interested. But she'd lost the habit of praying; she had to decide for herself now, first time ever. It was more than a little scary.

But what was that, ahead?

HAVE YOU SEEN ME?

Whole gallery of faces.

Dee Anna had passed many such notices in her time, tacked up on the walls of the post office and even at the grocery where she'd worked after school, but somehow they'd never really held her attention before. Those lost and missing children had been picture faces only. Now for the first time they came to her as living and breathing, fully real. Or at least the faces on the left struck her that way. Most of the faces were double; the ones on the left—how they looked before they'd gone missing; on the right—how they'd look today. There were two Tracys, two Garretts. A three-year-old girl with dimples named Precious, with just the one photo since she'd disappeared only last month. Others—Jayson and Gloria, both smiling—also too recent to have more than one picture apiece. There were two Russells, frowning in each, and two Kens, with hard mouths, lips pressed tight. There were two Ashleys.

Dee Anna was thinking that she couldn't recall a time when she'd ever really liked her name.

Ashley was the one she wanted to be. A name like that. Hair like that. DOB—that was date of birth. Same year as Dee Anna. But Ashley got away. Lucky Ashley. She'd been gone three years. The photo on the left, what she looked like before she went missing, was hard to see: whoever shot it must of been aiming straight at the sun. Dee Anna had to walk right up to the photo, nose to nose practically, to make out the details. Braces, first of all. She had to be a rich kid—who else gets braces? Blondish. No, very blond . . . fine ash-blond hair with bangs that hung straight down. Her eyebrows didn't hardly show, they were so fair. Around her neck she wore a heart locket on a thin chain. You couldn't really tell in a photo, but Dee Anna knew it was made of pure gold.

Ashley got away.

The picture on the right was what Ashley was supposed to look like now. It was sharp and clear but different from a photograph. Somebody made it up, a machine maybe, a computer. She did look older in this one—eyebrows tweezed, arched and clear, like she'd penciled them in. Eye shadow, lipstick. Her face was pointier, thinner, her smile less trusting. You couldn't see her teeth in this one to tell if her braces had done any good or not. Her hair, which lay flat in the first photo, was styled here, pulled back from her forehead and curled under at the ends. And she wasn't wearing the locket now. But how did they know all this if Ashley was missing? Who could say what she looked like today? Nobody. Could be she was fat now with hair spilled all over her face. Maybe her hair had turned dark, maybe she'd shaved it off or dyed it green. Nobody knew. Kids got lost all the time; it was easy because—unless you made trouble or a lot of noise—few people ever noticed you when you were standing right there in front of them.

They'd notice if she wasn't on that bus, though. They'd be sorry . . .

Oh, would they? Really? Sorry, how? She'd been the wipe-your-hands-on-the-dog person; she'd been the dog person. Dogs were loved better than she was.

She never again wanted to lay eyes on Jimmy or her stepbrother, Luke. She could just hear Jimmy bragging on what he'd done, the two of them, Luke and Jimmy, laughing their heads off. Let them! It couldn't touch her if she never went back to them. She had no love for her stepmom, none, never had; it was no secret: they put up with each other was all. And her dad had never been on Dee Anna's side. It was useless trying to tell him anything, she was always the one to blame. And it went way beyond blame. It got so she couldn't even make herself heard—teachers telling her to "speak up"—her voice so small and clotted, so unused, that it sounded like laryngitis the few times she really did try to make it carry.

It was then Dee Anna decided. Not so much a decision as letting things slide into place, how it felt. She'd change her ticket. Right then—while there still was time.

But—where to? She hunted around for a map and found a big one not far from the bank of telephones. Tracking with her finger, she located the red arrow saying YOU ARE HERE. It was pointing to this little speck off the main route. Duffy . . . What kind of name was that? She'd lived in Missouri all of her life and never heard of it. *You are here* . . . She continued standing in front of the map, her eye skidding east and north over state lines, roads, rivers. It looked so busy. She hadn't realized that there were so many roads, so many towns. She'd been acting like there was only one road on the whole planet. Greyhound routes, highlighted in blue, crisscrossed the map in all four directions. She had the whole country to choose from! But, wait—not so fast—she had fifty dollars, total, for whatever might be coming up. It was more money than she'd ever had in her whole life, but she'd never been on her own before. Out of state would be best, but not too far from Missouri. She noticed a town in Illinois called Starlight. She pressed her thumb to the spot so as not to lose it. Starlight, Illinois . . . But that was dreaming, of course; she knew she'd have to be practical now and choose a city of good size if she planned on getting lost in it.

Dee Anna wished a magic red dot would pop up somewhere to say, "Over here! Here's where you want to be."

Seemed like she recalled a woman being at the ticket counter when she'd entered the depot, but now it was a man who stood there. The clock over the ticket taker's head was moving in chunks; Dee Anna was all too painfully aware of it because her heart seemed to be beating to the same broken rhythm, moving in skips and bunches.

"Where you headed?" the man asked.

Dee Anna was going to explain about already having a ticket, hoping to exchange distance for distance, but decided not to bother. It would be worth the money not to have to explain anything. She'd pretend she was starting off here in Duffy. A clean break. And this way she'd be harder to track. She asked about stops in Ohio and the prices, and out of the blue, for no other reason than having to be quick and act like she knew what she was doing, she picked Columbus. Then she opened her folding money.

"Columbus," the ticket man smiled, "the new world."

A new world . . . I wish. Already Dee Anna knew better. Only the ticket was new. Tucking it into its envelope, she fumbled, her fingers clumsy suddenly.

And soon as she'd turned away from the counter, she was called back.

"Aren't you forgetting something?" the ticket man asked.

She was. Two quarters and a nickel. Not a whole lot but not at all smart when each and every penny counted.

SAM WAS LOSING COUNT OF HOW MANY TIMES HE'D rounded the perimeter of the waiting room. For the last few laps, he'd been paying particular attention to the jittery girl who'd recoiled and fled when he held open the door for her. Now she was at the ticket desk, double counting her money before handing it over. For the longest time before that she'd been standing and staring at a poster for missing children. Perhaps she recognized one of the faces. It occurred to Sam that the girl herself might be one of those faces—a runaway. Well, but supposing she were? What was he supposed to do about it? It was none of his business, really. He continued pacing.

ENOUGH TIME FOR A WASHUP? PLENTY, GOING BY THE overhead clock. Dee Anna could count on twenty minutes at least until the first boarding call.

But the girl at the next sink seemed to want the whole place to herself—with good reason. Dee Anna couldn't help noticing. The girl had peeled off her T-shirt and was busy soaping her neck, under her armpits and upper chest, one nipple pierced with a gold ring that matched the one in her lip. Dee Anna wanted to ask, "Doesn't it hurt?" But she already knew the answer: it was supposed to hurt. Hurting was the whole point. Suddenly the girl turned on Dee Anna, her face knotted up: "Do we have a problem here?"

Then Dee Anna shifted her focus to the sink, down to the deep center of the bowl, where gathered hairs were nesting.

"So why were you staring at me like that?"

Dee Anna let out a breathless "sorry" and cut her eyes away from the sink, stepping quickly through the door without even pausing to dry her hands. She moved like a ghost, the damp soles of her shoes screeching faintly. Ashley would handle it differently, Dee Anna felt sure. Ashley would face the girl down and slam right back at her with, "If you don't like being stared at, cover up!" Ashley would take her own sweet time rinsing and drying her hands, nobody pushing her around!

INSIDE THE BUS, FOOD ODORS MIXED WITH SWEAT, diapering, and bad sleep, curdled in the unmoving air. *Air so thick you could taste it . . .*

Although she knew this would be a long, leisurely rest stop (the most generous ones seemed to be given at the most ungodly hours), Eileen had decided not to get off the bus. She hated to watch people standing and eating for one thing. Eat and run was the fashion these days, even when you had time to spare. What was the rush? Where to? Cattle grazing in the fields had more dignity. More sanity overall.

So many customs these days grated on her; once started on the subject, Eileen could go on for weeks. She'd begin with the demise of letter writing—snail mail, as it was called now. The scarcer letters became, the more she treasured them. Real letters, crammed with news and homespun wisdom, the kind you tucked away to read again and again. She still wrote long, leisurely letters, devoting time, thought, and feeling to choosing her words, and that care extended even to her penmanship, her *l*'s and *g*'s always gracefully looped, but she'd long ago ceased to expect answers in kind.

Answering machines were another of her peeves. Eileen wouldn't permit one in her own house, no matter how much her children insisted. She couldn't avoid their machines, of course, but found herself constrained and resentful whenever she had to speak into one of them. What would be the point of her owning such a thing? If she were at home, she would answer; if not, she would not. She considered it more than rude not to answer the phone if you were at home and heard someone ringing. Even a salesman deserved that much consideration. Whatever became of courtesy?

Yes, she'd grown cranky, rigid, old. People lived too long these days. She'd overstayed. Here she sat, nobody beside her, nobody loved her . . . And yet she was grateful for the extra seat. Right now her back was bothering her. Badly. She'd need a visit to the chiropractor as soon as she got back home. For the time being, all she could do was to take advantage of the empty seat beside her to elevate her legs. Her ankles were swollen, and her right hip, the one she'd had to have pinned, might have been incandescent, the pain so flaunting. If only she were able to nap! But that was impossible, what with all her aches and pains and the overhead lights left on to make passage safe underfoot, the swooshing of the door as it opened and shut, the ceaseless coming and going.

At the moment, Eileen felt totally awake, yet only partially alive. That was age, of course, but also the hour. Two in the morning brought with it a mood like no other. *Why don't you take me out in the backyard right now and shoot me?* was the feeling. *Why wait?*

But Eileen couldn't—wouldn't!—abide it when she got this way. And she'd developed any number of strategies for combating the mood. There was the misery-everywhere-you-look, misery-loves-company approach; late-night talk shows kept her current on this. Another—completely opposite—was the relentlessly positive tack: *Think of all the good things in the world . . . Hold fast to what you already hold fast to.* And then there was her favorite: *When in doubt, sing*—something she'd gleaned from her last cataract operation.

Naturally, the operation hadn't been all singing. That happened only toward the end when, without warning, the machine for rinsing the eyes broke down—not a spurt to be coaxed out of it. Dr. Rossi set down his tools calmly. Lowering his mask and smiling gently, he'd announced: "I'm going to sing for you while we wait." And he did sing, in a rich tenor voice, full volume. Eileen was startled—stunned was more like it—she'd never associated surgery with singing.

Perhaps he was trying to signal help without frightening her, although Eileen heard no trace of panic or urgency in his voice. It was an old song, not a hymn, not unfamiliar, yet she couldn't summon up more than a phrase when she tried . . .

Silver hairs dumdum dum dum (must rhyme with old*) fold? . . . Enclose? . . . Mold? . . . Sold? . . . Or (what else could it be?)—gold? . . .*

Then it came to her:

> Darling, I am growing old,
> Silver threads among the gold . . .

And he kept on singing until—it seemed a second miracle, the song itself, the first—the rinsing machine started to sputter and cough. At once, Dr. Rossi put up his mask and, in silence, became an eye surgeon again . . .

Remembering, Eileen caught herself humming.

SOON THE FIRST BOARDING CALL WOULD GO OUT. SAM Shevra told himself it wouldn't be long now. The seemingly endless rest stop had not been restful, and Sam was eager to get going, maybe catch a little shut-eye this time, it ought to be possible. *If only they'd get started!*

Not far off from where he posted himself the usual smokers had gathered. They stood knotted together around the trash bin closest to the bus. Sam noticed the same clustering at every stop— the same motley figures pushing forward in a tearing hurry to be the first ones out the door. Gasping for a gulp of their poison . . . Didn't matter that they'd been forewarned that there wouldn't be enough time for a smoke; they'd go through the exact same charade, the same desperate last puffs, when the minute was up and the promised reboarding call came. Sam, for his part, hadn't smoked in over two decades. He felt pretty righteous about this. Reading the early statistics on lung cancer and smoking, he'd found the correlation convincing. He might be depressed from time to time, but he wasn't a life hater yet.

Not yet . . . Sam stared at the stranger approaching. Looked like something washed up on the beach. Like an advertisement for a long-since-faded summer in his yellow shorts and pastel T-shirt with bending palms and ghost-pink flamingos. Sam was struck by the figure's dead-white, wintry pallor. Too many happy hours, was it? Or too many blood donations for quick cash? But—*wait*—he was leaping to judgment again. The man could have been a traveler, it was possible. He wasn't necessarily homeless—no lawn bag or pillowcase for hauling his gear around. In fact, he had a neat blue bowling bag for carry-on; it was perfectly respectable. And his sneakers, though unlaced, were span white.

No, he was homeless, Sam could tell. His own bristling was the tip-off. And now—in two blinks—the man was in his face and Sam was sure: *Another deadbeat panhandling for change.*

But all the poor slob wanted, it seemed, was conversation. "Here's what I think," he blurted. He paused. Sam waited to hear more.

"Yes, what?" Sam asked irritably when the pause persisted. "What do you think?" The panhandler stared blankly back at him, as though he had no idea what Sam was talking about. He pulled absently at his crotch then turned and walked away.

Sam's gaze pursued the man as he wandered off to join the smokers huddled around the trash bin. From one he bummed a cigarette, from another a light. Lighting up, he dawdled, made a movie moment of it; he seemed to be sipping air from his palms, which were cupped round the hands of the man who held out the match to him. Others did not take kindly to this. One of them—a man wearing a bill cap with a mesh crown standing a full two inches above his skull, so his head seemed to be half air—was grumbling at the top of his voice: "Some of us have to *pay* for what we get!" But even after his cigarette was well alight, the panhandler took no notice of any unpleasantness, stalling there, in their midst, his gaze revolving slowly round the circle, moving carefully from face to face as if to memorize them, one by one. "Need us to suck it for you?" the bill cap put in. "Need a kick in the butt to start it sucking?" There was no mistaking the tone of this, and the panhandler took off. He made his way with painful slowness, as though wading. Then parked himself behind a pillar and stood there, cigarette dangling from his fingers, waiting for whatever promised or unpromised thing might yet be coming his way. At that moment, he seemed to Sam a young man—young but wasted. He could have been coming from the Caribbean or Florida, except for the fact of his extreme pallor. Sam noticed how swollen his ankles were. Although his face had the deep hollows and creases of age, he might have been twenty-five and ailing. He might have been suffering from AIDS. He took a long drag on his cigarette with eyes closed. Even the smoke he exhaled had a slow, lazy, almost-sullen drift.

He let it burn down to the nub before opening his eyes again. "Here!" The airhead flung another butt, still glowing, in the panhandler's direction. The panhandler's gaze marked its trajectory, shifting from the ground to the air at chest level, then back, avoiding their faces now. When he finally made a move, it was warily, testing the thing with the toe of his sneaker, drawing it slowly toward himself. The glow was long gone, the cigarette cold, by the time he stooped down to claim it. This time, he didn't bother to ask for a light, simply stashing the butt in the back pocket of his shorts for another occasion. It was then that Sam turned to notice the sad little girl in the too-big dress coming through the doorway, her expression perhaps a shade brighter than before. He wasn't distracted for long, a matter of seconds, but when he turned back, the panhandler was nowhere in sight. As if he'd evaporated into thin air . . .

AS SOON AS SASHA REJOINED CLEM, SHE'D COMMENCED tugging as before. Again, she wanted to go where the bright lights were—especially the twinkling, tweeting, bleeping lights from the video games, which ate up your money faster than you punched it in. The snack machines didn't flash or beep, but they swallowed money nearly as quick. Someone she'd met in the women's room had given Sasha a cinnamon candy—no favor as far as Clem was concerned. All it did was pepper her up and perk her appetite for more.

He had to keep yanking her away from the lights toward the dim boarding area. She balked, her shiny leather shoes planted to the floor—those ridiculous dress-up socks with their lacy cuffs . . . "Do what I say!" He had to shake her loose.

"Ain't gonna!"

"OK," he said, not knowing beforehand where he was going with this. "Guess I gotta sell you, then . . ."

"You ain't!"

What a nuisance she was! Sasha struggled to tug loose, but Clem held fast. Swiping one eye with her free hand, she started to whimper; in a minute, she'd be bawling.

"Just hush . . ."

He'd show her! Clem scanned the waiting room from corner to corner, searching for the man who'd offered to buy her. Not a trace. What he did find, and in desperation point to, was the passenger he'd been sitting beside. "See that one yonder?" The man was standing up against the door to gate 6, his wool cap pulled down to his eyebrows, headset dangling like a necklace. When Sasha, following Clem's pointing finger, saw what he meant for her to see, her whimper became a wail.

GLANCING OUT THE WINDOW, EILEEN SAW THE ODDEST thing. What looked, for all the world, like a clown; he was leaning against a pillar. He wore a pale pink top and yellow shorts. And big white stumblers—clown shoes—with trailing laces. He was dancing, aping dance, sliding one leg forward, swaying, drawing the foot back, then advancing the other leg in a half circle, swaying, drawing the foot back. He seemed to be taking his cues from the cluster of standing men who were gathered round a tall drum; they were blowing tiny flutes, lifting and pointing them in his direction as he stooped to touch his toes . . . Eileen had to turn away—they were baiting him, she felt certain of it. *But it couldn't be for real . . .* Her eyes must be playing tricks on her. She needed her sleep before dreams took over and invaded her waking space completely.

All That Road GOING

She couldn't close her eyes for more than a minute, though. Well before the call to reclaim their seats, the continuing passengers started trickling in. The reboarding soon became a free-for-all, and Eileen had no choice but to lower her swollen feet and squeeze over to one side, resigning herself to the fact that their rest stop—and with it her only chance of rest for the night—was over.

The reboarders seemed much the worse for wear—most of the men unkempt and stubble cheeked. Nearly everyone looked debauched: eyes heavily shadowed, vacant. The scruffy fellow in the knit cap swept by, a noisy passage. He was followed at a little distance by a young lady who'd clearly put her time to good use: rouge, eye shadow, lipstick. It struck Eileen as a great waste of effort, given the setting and the hour.

Then came the kids who were traveling on their own. The boy was dragging his sister up the steps. The girl arched back and away, struggling to get loose. With her free arm, she clung to the handrail, to the armrest of the front seat. Her face was raw, shiny with tears. And Eileen couldn't help reaching out, bending low so she was eye to eye with the child, asking, "What's the matter, honey?"

"He—mean to me," was all Eileen could make of her reply. The boy continued yanking his sister's arm to get her to move on, but the girl went on stalling despite him, her eyes fixed on Eileen.

"How about you sit up front with me awhile? You can have the window seat, would you like that?" When Eileen turned to ask the boy for permission, his eyes were elsewhere, as if he were no longer part of this scene.

"I don't care," he answered and let drop his sister's hand.

Snuffling, the girl squeezed past Eileen's knees and mounted the empty seat.

Eileen was so busy rummaging in her purse for a tissue that she failed to notice Dee Anna moving past, failed to catch her guilty mumble of greeting.

"Now blow, don't suck it back," Eileen urged. "Don't pick your nose—don't swallow it—just blow!" The child seemed to be getting the idea. She held the tissue to her nose but then sucked the mucus back and swallowed noisily, thrusting the crumpled tissue, still dry, into Eileen's hands. She turned after that, made kissing faces, flattening her face against the glass, then streaked her fingers across the pane, leaving faint, slimy smudges, like snail tracks. It was several minutes before Eileen was able to persuade her to stop decorating the window and speak her name. Then Eileen told Sasha what a pretty name, how unusual, and asked her age.

Sasha raised her right hand, folding two fingers down; that left three pointing up. "Oh, well, now, that can't be," Eileen said. "Aren't you forgetting your other hand?"

SAM SHEVRA AVERTED HIS HEAD WHEN THE MAN WHO'D stolen his soup passed him on his way down the aisle. Sam could have sworn that he was rattling his lunch box, knocking it against an armrest here and there, simply to add insult to injury. The way to deal with it was to ignore him, deny him the satisfaction. *Forget all about it*—Sam's face tensed in a wincing smile—the soup episode had been nothing if not ridiculous. Ridiculous, trivial . . .

Therefore—*forget it!*

DEE ANNA SPIED A FREE SPACE NEXT TO THE WITCHY GIRL with the spiky hair, who was at that very moment in the process of punching her backpack into a pillow before stretching her legs out. "Oh, jeez," she frowned at the intrusion. Here she'd come all the way from Barstow, California, and hadn't been able to stretch her legs in all that time. "Can't you find any place else?" she whined. "I'm wiped out."

Dee Anna could not speak. She was thinking of Ashley, how Ashley would shake her head forcefully, how Ashley wouldn't budge an inch about having it her way. But that wasn't really what kept her standing there. Dee Anna was too paralyzed to move, what it was; she had nowhere else to turn. If she couldn't sit here, she couldn't sit anywhere, because she wasn't going back to her old seat next to that chink with the roving hands and the book he used as a cover. It had to be this seat.

"Jeez . . . ," the girl muttered at last, making an ugly face as she cleared space for Dee Anna.

WATCHING THE GIRL RESETTLE WHERE, ANYONE COULD tell, she wasn't welcome, Dee Anna's former seatmate sighed: he didn't know what he'd done wrong. It was she who'd pressed to sit beside him. She'd been the forward one; he'd done nothing.

He'd come all the way from Karakul, a backwater town known, if at all, for the sheep of that name and for being only a short distance from Bukhara. He'd dreamed and worked all his adult life, more than fourteen years now, to be able to come to this country, this land of freedom and plenty. He'd avoided the old trades in cotton and silk and carpets, choosing instead to work on the trans-Caspian railroad, in a concrete factory, in auto-part sales; and looking ahead, always ahead, he managed to steer clear of marriage. But here in America at last, working off the book, living in YMCAs, hostels, and shelters, he found it all so different than expected. No one on this bus ever asked his name. His name was Rakhim Amin— not so very hard to say. True—he had been asked, twice in his long journey, but that was on another bus. Asking where he came from and hearing Karakul, the first man said, "That right?" But it was not any kind of question, because that was all he said. The second American who asked went farther: "Kara-who? Where's that?" He seemed to really want to know.

Rakhim tried his best to name something in his part of the world he thought the American might recognize. "Fergana Valley?" The American shook his head no. "Bukhara?" Same gesture.

"Samarkand, yes?"

"Maybe that one. In a fairy tale, could it be?" the American said. "Who'd of thought it was for real, though . . . Live and learn." And that was the end of that.

In this country everyone was supposed to be so friendly. When they told the news on the television they smiled; the advertisements were full of smiling faces—everybody so happy, their teeth always showing and shined and white. But that was only on the television and in magazines, not on this bus. On this bus, their teeth were yellow and gray and he'd seen one man, who wasn't old, mashing his food against his bare gums.

Perhaps it was his poor English. He was still only learning. People gave him so little chance to practice. But he would keep working on it, even so. He recalled his favorite sentence from all the other sentences in the book: "It is more important to see than to say." He mouthed it to himself. He pronounced this sentence so perfectly because he understood it, and because he believed it to be true.

Rakhim didn't feel like sleeping, so he took out his phrase book and let it fall open where it would. "*That was easy to arrange.*" He angled both overhead lights to meet on the same page. "*It is all in vain*" and it would help pass the time. "*Let's have a barbecue,*" he ran his finger over the line.

He would have liked to ask the girl how to say this word *barbecue*. And he wanted to hear her say *shoulder* and *pour*, how the same *ou* was a different sound, one from the other. And how to say *garden* and *gardenia*, and *button*—not *baton*. And why did *river bank* and *savings bank* have the one same word? One was money, one was water.

But none of this was what he wanted to know, really. What he really wanted to know was, what did he do wrong? He turned the book face down on his lap. Stooped over the shopping bag at his feet, digging for the special nougat he'd brought from home. There it was—calmative, sleep bringer, mender of sorrow—

hiding at the very bottom. He broke off a large chunk of it with his teeth, caressed it with his tongue, savored its dusty sweetness. Then he shut the book and waited.

But the calm he needed did not come. His thoughts returned to the same round. She was the forward one, not he.

Three

Construction

AS THEY'D PULLED OUT OF DUFFY, SAM SHEVRA FOUND himself scanning the loading platform for another glimpse of the panhandler. Nothing, though. It was the damndest thing—the man had vanished so suddenly.

Ghostly hour . . . The light leached out of everything. A string of pennants fluttered in the distance, signaling some festivity or used-car lot. Car lot, it turned out. The pennants, sure to be brightly colored by day, were ashen now, the cars gray toned, shades of lunar monochrome. Sam's gaze skimmed over a row of dark, shuttered houses, a long shelf of the single storied. The houses were detached, freestanding, each with a little smudge of lawn, yet it was hard to tell one from the next: here a birdbath, there a Virgin Mary, a flamingo, a FOR SALE sign, a swing, a sprinkler left spinning, the slow twist of water wasting itself on the night air.

Ahead SOUP—SAND beckoned in blue neon: an all-night diner apparently, interior lights undimmed. The place looked empty, though. *Come to think of it, a bowl of hot soup would have been nice . . .* Sam was hungry. Shaky as water and at the same time—how could it be?—parched.

. . . Chicken rice, it'd been, faint yellow, with no visible chicken and precious few particles of rice, yet the broth became a banquet, luscious, shimmering in his mind's eye, golden in regret.

Let it go. It's nothing—already forgotten.

But Sam's hunger persisted. And now, inexplicably, his fingers were starting to itch and to throb—as if scorched and blisters were forming. As if his own fingers had plunged into the steaming broth . . .

No use trying to sleep.

And to think that he'd pissed away all that money trying to beat the odds in Laughlin! Almost enough for an airline ticket or a down payment on an apartment in Pittsburgh . . .

He was so beat. Right now what Sam wanted more than anything was to hit the sack. But sleep was clearly out of the question. The closer he got to Pittsburgh the harder it would be even to rest. Where would he find the energy to start over again, or the clarity of mind he needed to make the right decisions when he arrived? There were too many questions facing him. The matter of start-up costs, for one. He didn't know whether to lease a van or a loft, whether to go to the customers or have them come to him. Flat lease or step lease or month to month? The infernal decision tree kept going fractal, springing branches, each branch a tree. Franchise or independent? He'd have to wait until he was situated to decide. Applying for a franchise would settle a bunch of worries in one fell swoop; there'd be more security, but fees and royalties would take a big bite out of what little savings he'd managed to scratch together so far. Plus he didn't think he could stomach having to put up with someone else's half-baked formulas and procedures, knowing how doubtful the chemistry behind them. More than likely he'd be starting out as an independent again. Just another jackleg operator, one of hundreds on the market, despite having three diplomas to hang on the wall. Diplomas and the know-how, a concept—not many in the business had the foggiest. The process he'd developed was his trade secret, a chem-dry formula without steaming or shampooing, no shrinkage, none of that endless waiting for a sodden carpet to dry. Speedy drying time was his selling point, a matter of hours instead of the usual two to three days. He'd have to keep abreast of the EPA's latest on chemical hazards. Too many products on the market nowadays were covered over with citrus fragrance, as if that would undo the toxicity. And, oh yes, he'd have to beef up his insurance, might need to add a malpractice provision, wouldn't surprise him, people being so much more mistrustful and litigious in the big cities of the East . . . But—he had solid chemistry behind him, Sam kept coming back to that. And he did intend to do a proper search and apply for a patent on his formula after he got really settled, when and if . . . If only he could think of anything more than how to scrape by, he might be able to think, actually think, for a change. It would be a hell of a note once he did get around to doing a search, only to find that his concoction was not that original or new. Or worse: already obsolete . . .

The bus crept through the deserted streets, observing all the traffic signs, although most of the stoplights were only blinking at this hour and there was no one around to care one way or the other. Houses, buildings, blew by. They went down a street where everything was under construction—construction or demolition, hard to say which. They passed an industrial park, a sprawl of warehouses, sheds, and loading docks, and at last arrived at the access road to the highway. Car lights, red and white, flicked past them: on the pike, at least, people were moving. The bus steadily gained speed, the motor hummed. Suddenly, the panhandler's face bloomed at Sam's side, afloat in the blackened lake of the window pane. But, *wait* . . . That couldn't be—the man would have to be clamped to the side of the bus. It was Sam's own face coming back at him, the ghost of his own reflection; he hadn't recognized himself.

Sam shut his eyes, hoping to banish the reflection. But there it was, that other face, the one he only imagined he'd seen in the window pane. The cheeks' concavities deepened, the image sharpened. He saw the panhandler approach the huddle of smokers to beg for a cigarette, then for a light, saw him stall, unwanted, in their midst after the light took hold. Why did he linger there?

Sam had to wonder: why should he be so irked—so haunted—by the man? His encounter with the panhandler had been momentary. He'd lost nothing by it, not a cent; there'd been no physical contact between them . . . Yes, but some contact had been made. A recognition, almost a salute—*hey there!* But this was absurd. The man had nothing in common with Sam—who worked, who struggled, who never begged. Who played by the rules always. The difference between them was glaring. The panhandler had nothing to do with him, nothing at all. Why, then, was Sam so put off, so personally affronted, so interested in such a person?

And furthermore, wasn't this a displacement? Conflating the panhandler with that other fellow (*again!*) who'd stolen his soup—the one who (futile to pretend otherwise) really rattled him? The one who made his fingers sting, even now?

Not rational!

The last of the overhead lights blinked off. Voices faded. Except for one—in midsection, someone's high-pitched, adenoidal snoring; his mere breathing sounded full of argument, complaint. The driver wasn't chatting anymore but fully occupied, packing the miles in, one eye on the speedometer, one roving. Looking out for the company rep, as he'd explained to Sam: "He could be riding this bus. He could be anyone. He could be you—I'd only find out after." Their speed was dizzying to Sam, like channel surfing, the passing scenes as little real. Lights, signs, buildings flashed forward and were withdrawn as quickly. Then—out of nowhere—obstruction loomed.

And then it was upon them, with lane shifts and a detour promised a mile up the road. The signs said, ROAD WORK and REDUCED SPEED. They went down to fifty-five on cue; half a mile later it was forty-five; the driver sighed as he downshifted; then thirty-five, crawling along in second. Sam was willing to bet the

All That Road GOING

signs were left over: somebody forgot to pull them; from all he could see, whatever construction had been underway was already completed. And even if that weren't the case, there wouldn't be any work going on at this hour. The driver wasn't taking any chances, though.

Single file now—this huge arrow in pulsing lights, left lane ending, a torchlight procession of glowing orange cones. Sign coming up: DO NOT PASS. An RV, solid as an armored tank, swerved sharply into their lane, trunk to nose—nearly grazing the side mirror of the bus. Both horns blatted at the same moment.

"Pass—pass—be my guest," the driver hissed. "What's the advantage—being one car up? It's cra-zy!"

"It's criminal!" Sam answered with a vehemence that surprised him—it was so out of proportion. "That guy's willing to kill for it . . ."

Concrete road barriers for the next ten miles, almost no shoulder to speak of, the driver too busy concentrating to converse, only muttering to himself, "Wasn't a thing in the world wrong with this road day before yesterday . . ." Sam returned to his solitary brooding.

Funny about life stories . . . how it was only a strand at a time that got teased out and told, never the full weave. When Sam was telling the driver his own story, he'd left out a crucial detail. What he didn't say was: it was all that space in Arizona wearing him down, all that road going, all that sky. All that sun . . . and an ache that could not be solarized. He didn't say how he'd fled, hiding out in library reading rooms, soaking up darkness in movie theaters, courting physical exhaustion (hoping to sleep after) by turning lap upon lap round the grand concourse at the mall. "Just schlepping, not shopping," he'd ward off an overzealous salesgirl, her counter spread with men's accessories, women's notions, whatever—it was all a bright blur to him. He didn't smoke, yet might as well have, since wherever he went he made the air unbreathable. And yes, he'd tried for some other way, even dated a couple of times—the kind of women a carpet cleaner would date—and, sure, he knew he was no prize. He'd carried through the little ceremonies of asking out—dinner, drinks, conversation, reminding himself: *eye contact, make an effort, look interested*—but could hardly keep the woman in focus. Somewhere, maybe half an hour, an hour into it, came the inevitable disconnect—*why am I doing this?* Being alone was easier. Or if not easier, more honest, that was the trade-off.

Pulse

HEAD ACHING, CLINGING TO HIS DREAM BY THE THINNEST of threads, Pierson awakened. Felt like his head was bursting through glass. But the dream had started off peacefully enough . . . something about a lake, the lapping of water. He'd been wading to his thighs . . . What else? Keeping his eyes shut and holding fast to the thread, he tried to move back, inch over inch, to re-enter the water of the dream . . .

He'd been fishing, reeling the line in, he'd just landed a big one, bass maybe; the hook was deeply embedded, he needed a knife to pry it loose, but soon as he regained the shore, the fish was flapping, thrashing back into the deep, the water swallowing everything, fish, line, lure, leaving only a thin trail of blood in its wake.

And then he—Pierson—was stepping out of Marie's room, he heard her calling after him and he was racing down a hallway tiled like a swimming pool in watery aquamarine. Past an open doorway, where the man in the white coat nodded and winked and waved his stethoscope aloft, waving him on, and as the doctor's door slammed shut, the door at the end of the corridor opened by itself and Pierson stood side of the highway in a blinding glare. And then he was running, running in place, trucks hurtling past him, his feet pounding—

That's all he remembered.

Pierson opened his eyes. He was sitting, not running, but his heart was pounding. Instead of the blazing, open sky, he found himself in a place of shadows. Dead air. He stared at the dense shape of the man beside him, trying to place the stranger. Trucker, wasn't it? No . . . That was the other one, the one from before. Two rows up, some old crone was going on and on. Sounded like she was trying to reason with a deaf child, when anyone with an ounce of sense would have quit trying hours ago. It was too dark for lip-reading or sign language, so why not give up, go to sleep?

Go to sleep!

Aside from the old woman and the deaf kid, everybody seemed to be sleeping. Nothing but row after row of huddled, faceless figures around him. The soft thudding of the tires, the beat of rubber on smooth asphalt, was oddly soothing, a lapping sound, as regular as the stroking of oars in the waters of a lake. If only his head would quit throbbing! The gnawing pain had its own crazy on-again, off-again rhythm, nothing to do with the measured lapping of the tires.

He must have been gnashing his teeth, what it was. Hadn't done that since he'd had nightmares as a kid. That went way back . . . Poking around with his tongue, Pierson discovered that, sure enough, he'd actually taken a bite out of himself—a real chunk, a flap of flesh from the tender lining of his cheek hung loose and it was bleeding—that's what was aching.

Commotion

"WHEN I WAS YOUR AGE . . ." EILEEN WAS RECALLING HER favorite games. She tried to make herself clearer by adding, "When I was just as little as you are," but this was no better. Sasha gave her such a squint that Eileen dropped the subject then and there.

When her grandkids were small, Eileen was in the habit of telling them, "I know all about little girls" or "I know all about little boys." She'd had two of each, after all, but nothing she knew seemed to apply to this particular little girl. With Sasha, Eileen had to admit she didn't know the first thing.

She was a cutie, no question; yet there was a problem, something distinctly not all right there. A habit of leaving her mouth hanging open, for one thing, as if her tongue were too big to rest comfortably in its socket. Added to that was her incessant fidgeting and rocking. And heaven knows, it was hard enough to keep a normal child quiet and amused these days. Sasha's continual jiggling, though, went way beyond restlessness.

The only thing that succeeded in holding her attention for longer than a heartbeat was Eileen's hand. With her tiny forefinger,

Sasha traced the branching veins and liver spots. Over and over, this mute, probing gesture. Then she asked Eileen who made the "writing" on her hand.

How to explain?

"Time writes," Eileen tried, "that's what time does." It sounded ridiculous, even to her own ears. And, really, she needn't have bothered—already Sasha had lost interest. Now the child was entirely occupied in a sort of sitting dance, rocking backward and forward, side to side.

By dint of the greatest patience, Eileen had managed to learn a few things. That her brother's name was Clem; that they were traveling to—she couldn't say the place. After one sleep, they were going to the zoo with the same auntie who was coming to get them at the bus. Sasha loved kittens a lot but bunnies best because they didn't scratch or bite you. Clem was mean to her, she kept coming back to that. Every time she repeated Clem's name, tears came, her old sorrow bubbled up.

What to do? Eileen was stumped. Did Sasha know any songs? "Row, Row, Row Your Boat"? How about "Old Macdonald Had a Farm"? No, not the McDonald with the Big Mac and the toys. "No? Well, how about 'Eentsie Weentsie Spider'?" This was probably not a good idea—who knew how she felt about spiders? . . . "How's that? Barney? Sorry." Eileen had to confess that she'd never learned the Barney song. She knew who Barney was, of course, you'd have to be blind not to. Television created him, and by now he was everywhere, on cups and toothbrushes, T-shirts and coloring books, that purple and green blimp of—but *what* he was Eileen never had been able to say. A dinosaur? He seemed only half formed, whatever he was intended to be, boneless, cushiony soft, his smile positively squishy sweet. Surely, and this must be the point: Barney was meant as a cure for monster anxiety; he—and he equally well might have been a she—was so thoroughly defanged, the nicest monster you'd ever want to meet . . .

Would Sasha like to teach her the Barney song?

Sasha would; she piped right up with it. The lyrics were blurry, something about love. *You, me,* and *fam-e-lee* seemed to be the rhymes. Even with repetition, the song lasted less than half a minute. Now Sasha wanted to see what Eileen kept in her handbag, and Eileen, fresh out of ideas, agreed to show her. No, Sasha couldn't poke around in another person's purse on her own, no, no, it wasn't nice, you simply could not do that.

What interested Sasha most was, no surprise, the thimble—the silver thimble Malcolm had given her after the birth of their first child, Gary. She'd used it with all four of her brood; when her kids were infants and teething, she'd cover one of her fingers with the thimble and let them chomp on it; it eased their itching gums. Lately, with her children long grown—past middle age, in fact, their infant selves vanished as if they'd never been—she needed to touch the thimble to recall those times, to prove to herself that those infants ever existed. And at the moment, she had a bit of work on her hands trying to explain to Sasha what a thimble was. Yes, it looked like a little cup, it sure did; but no, it wasn't for drinking . . .

When Eileen suggested she go fetch some of her toys, Sasha's face brightened. She was off at once, pushing roughly past Eileen's knees. It was then, her foot accidentally knocking against it, that she discovered the hatbox. She wanted to know what toys were hiding inside. Eileen assured her it was full of old socks. But wasn't Sasha going to show off her own most favorite toys as she'd promised? How about it?

While she was away, Eileen shoved the hatbox as far back under the seat as it would go. She wondered how the cake was faring, but there wasn't much she could do about it in any case. She had her doubts about whether Sasha would actually return or whether she'd find someone more appealing than an old lady who'd never learned the Barney song. But Sasha did return and speedily. And she seemed to have forgotten all about the hatbox.

She'd fetched a doll and a toy cell phone. They passed the phone back and forth between them. Eileen had never seen the like. When she pressed the operator key, a voice came on asking, "Can I hug you?" Pound: a cat's meow. Sasha pushed buttons randomly; she didn't seem much interested in make-believe conversation and quickly switched over to the doll. The doll's name was Kim. Kim was walking, she explained, poised on her tiny feet, Sasha's hand rocking the legs from side to side, across her own lap and continuing over onto Eileen's.

"Where's she going?" Eileen asked.

"Mmah-mah!"

"Does she miss her mommy?"

The question sparked fresh tears and the old refrain: "Clem— mean to me."

Eager to grasp at anything by way of escape from this sore subject, Eileen said, "See the stars?" pointing out the window to what might have been a dusting of snow on dark cloth. Sasha's answering stare did not reach beyond Eileen's finger at first. Then she seemed to grasp the idea, tapping Kim's face against the glass so the doll could see, too.

"Star light . . . Star bright," Eileen persisted, "first star I see tonight . . ." How did the rest go? There was a wish in it somewhere, of that she was sure. The rhymes—*light, bright, night*— ought to have clued her in. Yet nothing further came, her mind a total blank. Not that it mattered to Sasha or anyone else, but to Eileen, always on the alert for signs of decline, the least forgetting was no small concern.

Right at the moment, though, it was hard to concentrate on anything. From the back of the bus came a rising hum of voices.

Useless to try and reason with Sasha: "Yes, that was somebody yelling, but never mind." Sasha had already scrambled to her feet and about-faced. She was holding on to the headrest with both hands. Eileen had to lean sideways to brace the child in case the driver were to brake suddenly.

What now?

Something going on. More voices. Now Eileen herself was twisting round, straining to see.

Eileen and Sasha weren't the only ones. Up and down the length of the aisle, people were rubbernecking, hands thrust up for reading lights, heads craning. Gawking at nothing, since there was nothing but themselves to be seen. There were more than a few passengers standing, waiting in line for the restroom, that was all.

If ever, later on, she were depositioned to give an account of what happened, Eileen would have to say that things started off innocently enough. Somebody taking forever in the toilet, people lined up in the aisle waiting—none of it unusual. Finally, this rather large woman in a purple running suit took it upon herself to come forward and confront the driver.

At first the driver was full of good commonsense reasons for his not getting involved. He suggested that the woman try again. Try knocking a little harder and speak directly through the key-hole—whoever was inside might be hard of hearing. Give the person inside a minute or two more. The driver wanted to know whether she'd noticed any smoke coming through the crack under the door. She was fairly sure she hadn't but promised to make a point of double-checking when she went back there.

So that was how things stood. The driver adjusted his interior rearview mirror. He picked up his microphone. If the door failed to open within three minutes, he warned, he'd have to pull over, park the bus, and deal with the problem in person. And if that happened, they'd all suffer from the delay. He made his final offer with volume at full blast, making sure his voice carried to whoever it was walled up in the toilet.

"This is my final offer," he announced. "If you have ears . . ."

NERVES RAW, PIERSON STOOD SECOND IN LINE, CLUTCHING the back of a chair, waiting for the door to open. It was a solid chunk he'd taken out of his cheek. He felt rotten; he couldn't spit, so he'd been swallowing saliva laced with blood, his otherwise empty stomach going queasy with the mixture. He didn't have to take a leak, it wasn't that kind of emergency. But he badly needed to spit in private and to use a mirror to get a good look inside his mouth and assess how much damage he'd done to himself. What in hell was holding things up?

Standing there in the aisle, swaying with the motion of the bus, Pierson feared he was going to be carsick. People were already staring at him. *Tune them out!* And he tried: when he closed his eyes, everything around him faded . . . Something gleaming had his full attention. A needle—Pierson recognized what it was at once. Marie had pricked the tip of her finger, winced, dropped a stitch, recouped it, dropped it again, recouped again. Dropped it. Her laboring hands, now empty, let fall . . .

DEE ANNA, STANDING NEXT IN LINE, CONTINUED TO ARGUE with herself: it was simply the sudden change in temperature; she was just imagining things . . .

But, no, this was for real. The tightness, the wet. It wasn't supposed to happen, but here it was. Didn't matter what anybody said or how many pills she swallowed. With her arms drawn tight across her chest nothing gave her away as yet, but if she had to wait much longer, the whole sorry story would spill out of her for all the world to see. She needed to stock up on toilet paper, as much as she could stuff in her bra.

And, added to everything else, she was hungry. She needed something to fill her up inside.

EILEEN HAD A CRIMP IN HER NECK FROM TRYING TO SEE what Sasha was seeing and to keep her from falling. The child was still standing on the seat, her attention riveted for once. By now the inside lights were blazing. The driver had ordered those waiting in the aisle to sit back down—any place vacant would do for the time being—and warned those who'd never left their seats to stay put. His voice was stern, explaining that circumstances had forced his hand; he had no choice: he'd have to pull over and park and deal with the situation.

At least it was a good, wide shoulder he picked out, Eileen noticed. Even so, all it took was one drunk or sleepy driver. No

All That Road GOING

place side of the road was safe so late at night; this was a major highway. Fewer trucks and cars on it than earlier, true, but every one of them racing to beat the dawn.

Not safe, no.

There was a pause, as close to silence as this crowd could muster. The driver braked, cut the engine, raised himself from his seat. As he pressed forward, making his way down the aisle, the voices resumed, lapping like small waves in his wake.

The driver knocked first, bent his eye to the keyhole, flattened his ear against the door, then, shaking his head, drew back, reporting that he couldn't hear a thing. He rattled the latch—nothing again—and worried a bunch of keys out of his pocket. One by one, he tested them; one or two seemed almost to fit, but none did the trick. That's when he lost it—yelled out: "Hey! Somebody die in there?"

He was heaving his weight against the door when one of the passengers, a hefty young man, disregarding the order to stay put, rose from his seat and joined him. Together they heaved: no use. Two other passengers followed suit. Nothing budged.

WHEN I REALIZED I HAD TO QUIT DRIVING AND HAUL myself on back there, I was royally pissed. Pardon my French, but I'd gone beyond reason. I was so irked. "OK," I announced, turning up the PA system to full blast, "now I stop the bus . . ." Like what I had on my hands was a bunch of four-year-olds cutting up.

Told myself: *I can handle this.*

But then, so help me, I reached for my driver's cap before starting down the aisle, as if I couldn't do it on my own, as if that tin-whistle badge on my cap would make a deal of difference to whoever happened to be holed up in the toilet. The passengers did hush as I went by, though; I had their full attention now.

I made a big point of clearing the aisle and jangling my keys as I approached that door. It was all bluster, of course. To start with: I didn't have the key to the restroom, some damn-fool regulation never explained to me, which I didn't have the sense to ask about at the time.

I drilled my eye to the keyhole: Nothing. I sniffed. I couldn't smell smoke or anything. I tried my best to listen through the door for any clue to what was going on inside there. Were those plinking sounds I heard, or were my ears idling, tweaking my brain? Trying another tack, I called through the keyhole: "You all right in there? Can you give us a holler?"—thinking to start out conciliatory, don't you know. What I got back was more of the same nothing for my pains.

Then I went through the pretense of trying to find the right key, rattling the bunch and uselessly jamming one after another into the lock as far as they'd go. One went in all the way, a promising start, then refused to turn. After that, I started throwing my weight against the door. A fellow I'd ordered back to his seat a minute before stood up and joined me, another followed suit, and I must admit I was grateful. Far as we could tell, it wasn't only the lock that stood in our way. Whoever was inside seemed to be leaning against the door.

It was possible, though unlikely, that some kid had gotten himself locked in and was too scared to move. I'd had that happen before, but with kids you could count on plenty of noise—tears, screams, and such. Anyway, far as I could see, no kids were missing.

"All right, you!" I was shouting at that point, couldn't help myself. "I'll get the police to handle this. If that's what you want! You hear? They can take this door down in ten seconds flat." There was no answer. I made one last offer, talking, not shouting, one last try: "You can still save yourself a heap of trouble if you come out right this minute." *Yourself—and us,* I thought.

I jiggled the handle and pushed one final time. And then—I'm only human, and I'd been driving too many hours at a stretch—I kicked that door. Two more kicks for good measure. I gave the door a final heave . . .

"Hey—how about giving us a break? I'm asking nice now." And louder, "I won't next time."

But nothing.

Maybe somebody had died in there! It struck me when I'd leaned against the door that what I was feeling was an adult's dead weight—either that or somebody pressing back with all his might from the other side, I couldn't tell.

I must admit that my first thought was that it was the fellow in the wool cap, busy gunking up the works inside.

But that just shows how the mind runs on. He was doing nothing of the kind. There he was—blending in with the others for a change, part of the audience, head angled sharp right, eyes wide, taking in all the details. Listening hard, too, I bet, no longer pretending deaf, dumb, and blind. Everybody was awake, on full alert, by then. Talk, what there was of it, was pretty hushed.

Too many violent things—crazy things!—going on in the world. I'd have to call in, ask for a police escort to meet us at the nearest town. That should be—what?—Tule? Or Graham? Graham, I guessed. I'd have to check the map.

I made my return to the front slowly, taking a headcount while I was at it. Total: fifty-two. But how could that be? I retraced my steps, front to back. Fifty-two again, my original total. Fifty-two was exactly right.

Then—who was in the restroom? You couldn't lock the door except from inside.

And then, dammit, I knew! It had to be a stowaway. I consulted my map: Graham was too far, so I dialed ahead to the largest nearby town—Redmont. The first question the dispatcher there put to me was the same one I'd asked: "Sure there's no smoke?" I told him what my eyes told me. So OK, he agreed, Redmont would be ready for us, and I promised to be there in minutes, if nothing erupted in the meantime.

The Cause
of It All

THE DISPATCHER IN REDMONT WAS AS GOOD AS HIS WORD.
A full crisis-response team. My first impression was that this
was overdoing it just a bit, we're all so infected with the movies.
Only thing they needed was a SWAT troop in a crouch, ready
to breach, danger music building in the background. I was still
expecting—hoping—this wasn't going to turn out to be anything
more than a case of an ornery customer refusing to abide by the
rules. But—can't be too careful nowadays—*better safe than sorry.*
I had to admit that the idea of somebody holing himself up with
a bomb in there had crossed my mind, yet, knowing my clientele
as I did, it was far more likely that he (assuming it was a he)
had locked himself in the toilet to take a nip, a snort, a hit of
something he shouldn't. But anyway . . .

There they were, ready and waiting, as we came in. Squad car
with roof lights spinning, fire truck, ambulance. Some kind of dis-
posal wagon, looked like a well on wheels. No sign of the deputy
sheriff. Instead three cops, plus dispatcher, plus what looked like a
mechanic in a grease suit, crowbar in one hand and a cutting torch

in the other. Plus another special kind of mechanic—something to do with explosives, I guessed—in hard hat, mask, soft body armor, with this enormous toolbox resting beside him, a mirror on a long handle atop of it. Another thing that struck me right off the bat: the police were wearing rubber gloves—that's how ready.

Minute I opened the bus door, the dispatcher hopped on board, commandeering the PA system and ordering the passengers to exit the bus quickly and quietly. Also, a word of advice to stay clear of the bus—if anything happened, they'd been warned, the company would not be responsible. His final word was to listen for the reboarding call in half an hour or so when "all this unpleasantness" would be over.

Only one rough spot in an otherwise calm and orderly evacuation: the outsize woman in the purple running suit trying to elbow her way forward, saying, "Let's move it!" and "Trying to get by!" Until the man in front of her about-faced and let her have it: "Everybody's trying to get by here! Think you're the only one?" And harsher words went flying up and down the line. It was single file, one passenger following on the heels of another; the only way to clear the aisle was to press forward from whatever position you entered the line, no space for wedging in between or leapfrogging ahead. This was obvious to everyone except the lady in purple.

Soon as the passengers cleared out, the crisis team clambered on board. The masked mechanic trudged noisily to the rear, the man with crowbar and cutting torch following at a slight distance.

SAM SHEVRA GUESSED WHO THE TROUBLEMAKER WAS right away. He was pretty sure it was the crotch puller who'd approached him at their last stopping place. Trying to hitch a free ride by hiding out in the washroom, then slipping into one of the regular seats when the bus was well underway. It was a mystery to Sam, why anyone so vulnerable would take the risk. For the sheer joy of beating the system? How could one town have any advantage over another if you've nowhere to lay your head when you get there? Just another squat, another depot, one no different from the next, and more days of scrounging, hiding out, waiting. Waiting—for what?

THE DOOR WAS ABOUT TO BE LIFTED OFF ITS HINGES. Everything laid out on the floor: jamb spreader, bolt cutter, electric drill. I chose to remain on board—loyal captain, idle—at the wheel. From my post, I watched the experts go through their paces. Most of the passengers had marched themselves inside the terminal, as instructed; once inside, they gathered on the other side of the glass panels, peering back at us. A number of others who'd ignored the dispatcher's advice remained outside, though standing at a distance, ready to dash into the street if need be. Anything to catch a piece of the action, I suppose. The kid who'd been traveling with his little sister was part of this audience; I was thankful at least that his sister wasn't with him. I assumed that the old lady who'd taken her in hand had led her safely indoors.

Right at the moment, though, those two kids weren't my prime concern. I spotted the man in the knit cap standing outside with the bolder passengers; he'd positioned himself somewhat apart from the others. But there was nothing I could do about any of them at this point—they'd all been warned.

Like I said, my mind was elsewhere. The mechanics, ready to tear the door off, had my full attention. They'd barely touched the door with their tools, when—last thing I expected—the latch clicked, the door quietly opened. The game was up.

Turned out, I'd never laid eyes on the man who stepped out. If he had a ticket, I'd never seen it. I don't think I'd have forgotten him if he'd come aboard in the usual way. *Lordy!* He looked like something left over from the summer before the summer before, togged out in pastel shorts and T-shirt and white sneakers too big for him, worn without socks, laces untied. And he was deathly thin and pale, so right away I thought: *AIDS.* But I didn't have enough time to take in more details—the police were already pouncing on him, left and right, forcing his hands together, yanking them behind his back, snapping on cuffs. He yelped with the pain; they

All That Road GOING

had his arms bent, locked high up on his back, and he was arching backward, straining for relief. He kicked at the legs of the seats, trying to stall, as they dragged him down the aisle.

And all the while words streamed from him. Hard to make any sense of them—except for the loud *ticket* and the fainter *luggage*. The group halted—the stowaway in that painful arched-back posture—as one of the mechanics retraced his steps to the washroom. "Ticket, sure, I bet!" I heard him mutter as he went by.

Another wait-and-see as the mechanic adjusted his mask and proceeded to poke inside the washroom, first using the mirror with the long handle, then another device I didn't recognize, and finally his hands, thickly padded as they were. "This your luggage?" he held aloft what looked like a bowling bag with a logo from, of all things, Air Canada. Couldn't have been too heavy, judging from the loose and easy way he lifted it.

Back to marching. Quickstep this time, down and out and off to the side of the bus, the handcuffed man all the while protesting that he was a regular passenger, that he had a ticket, what an insult this was. Then, words making no dent, he started up kicking again. At that the cops muscled in, laid the man out flat, flat as he would go, half hog-tied as he was, handcuffed side up, face to the ground. Down to business now: Where did he say his ticket was? Had he *eaten* it by mistake? Playing along, don't you know, as if there really was a ticket to be found. They seemed to enjoy the game, this hide-and-seek, as they rummaged through his pockets and emptied out what he called his luggage, the bits of trash he'd squirreled away inside, and—no surprise to anyone— the ticket wasn't there.

As the man officially in charge, I must admit how embarrassed I was by the whole episode. My own oversight, first off. How come I hadn't noticed the man slip on board?

SAM SHEVRA WAS ONE OF THOSE BYSTANDERS WHO disregarded the dispatcher's advice, remaining outside, unable to tear himself away.

It had to be one of the saddest spectacles ever . . . the pan-handler forced face to the ground, his worldly goods spilled out on display in front of everyone. There was a ratty gray sweatshirt and some grayish underwear; a sparkling new (probably lifted) pair of white athletic socks, still in its plastic wrap; a bunch of lawn bags; plastic spoons, straws, couple of ketchup packets—all freebies. A half-eaten hamburger. A coat hanger bent, for some purpose, into the shape of a hook—simply one more useless item, as far as Sam could tell. In the old days hangers were bent like that to pry up the door buttons on locked cars, but most cars had electronic power locks these days—at least any car worth pilfer-ing had them.

And then—the very last item to tumble—what was it? A rub-ber bone? Chew toy, could it be? For a nonexistent pup?

They were all such useless—harmless—things.

The police poked at the swatch of lawn bags with the rein-forced toes of their boots. Even though gloved, they seemed to go out of their way to avoid touching anything. "Where'd you say your ticket was?" one of the officers asked for the umpteenth time. When the man on the ground failed to reply, the officer did stoop down to him, but only to yank at his handcuffs; you'd think the answer could be dragged out of the man through his wrists.

Sam was on the verge of blurting out—his throat ached, a palpable ache, so heavy with holding in. *Backwash* . . . His lips formed the word silently. This was the system at work. You took a person with few skills (but who knew whether this man had any skills at all?), surplus him, send him out to fend for himself, a person who doesn't even know how to beg, and leave him high and dry out on the streets. Then grind him to pulp when he tries to rejoin the flow.

The man on the ground had started up again, insisting that he had a ticket—if it wasn't in the bag then "must of dropped out, or somebody stole it"—when Sam knew, anybody could tell, there never was a ticket, never any question of a ticket. Who did he think was fool enough to believe him?

Man on
the Ground

EILEEN LEFT THE BUS WITH SASHA FIRMLY IN TOW. THEY
were headed for the ladies' room, always a good idea when
traveling but not, as it happened, so very good at that moment.
First thing they saw was a toddler standing near the sink. He was
naked, had done something messy, and was being toweled down
roughly by an old woman, probably his grandmother, tried beyond
her patience. She was yelling at him to hold still or she'd smack
his wee-wee off. Sasha, staring pointedly, grew very quiet, clearly
fascinated by the boy's tiny penis with its foreskin dripping down
from it like tallow. Eileen had to drag her off into one of the stalls
and position herself against the door, guarding it. Sasha, astraddle
a commode much too big for her, kicking its flanks, complained
that she couldn't do anything. Eileen said, "Try!" and Sasha said
it wouldn't come, but Eileen said, "Try anyway, I'm willing to
wait." Eileen was adamant by then, although she'd rather have
been almost anywhere else—the place was awful.

Suddenly the woman in the next stall cried out, "Praise the
Lord!" amid the sound of generous splashing, prompting a thin

trickle from Sasha; then her trickle gave way to a flow. By the time Sasha was done and they returned to the sink, the messy toddler and his grandmother had disappeared.

Back in the waiting area, the drift toward the glass doors was inevitable. And there was nothing Eileen could do, really, to stop herself from peeking. She recognized the man on the ground at once as the clown, the dancer with bright shoes and dangling laces she'd spotted at their last rest stop—she hadn't dreamed him up. But he was a stowaway, homeless probably. A street person, not a clown. No longer dancing, he moved very little. The men who stood around outside watching were passengers from her own bus.

Hard to believe how one of those passengers leaned forward now, aiming his camera lens at the man on the ground. He was using a flash; his picture taking was no secret. The officials were too busy, apparently, to take notice.

The man with the camera took three shots the long way, two the wide. Souvenirs, Eileen guessed. It would liven up the story he'd tell when his trip, his big adventure going cross-country, was over.

Eileen herself could not help but stare. The stowaway was twisted on his side; his cuffed hands were cranked too high up on his back, he couldn't lie flat. You could see, even if you couldn't hear, his open mouth working, words and spittle bubbling from his lips. Five men surrounded him, their legs staked like fence posts.

"Bad boy?" Sasha asked.

All Eileen could come up with by way of reply was, "He's hurting."

Then his face lifted toward Eileen, eyes blinking fast, like some trapped animal who'd been blindsided and stunned. There was a scrim of white at the corner of his lips, and it occurred to Eileen that maybe all he'd been doing when he locked himself in the washroom was something as innocent as trying to brush his teeth. But almost immediately upon thinking this, she noticed how hollowed his cheeks were—it was doubtful he had any teeth to worry about.

Restless again, Sasha tugged at Eileen's hand, and Eileen, wanting no part in the shaming of anyone, was all too willing to let the child pull her away from the door, to be led anywhere else.

They halted at the sight of a young woman in tights doing knee bends and stretches. She was at the head of the lineup for the Detroit bus and the first to move on through when the door opened. Sasha wanted to know why she and Clem and Eileen weren't going along, too.

What next? The shop selling souvenirs and magazines had a metal grille pulled down over the display window. Only the interminable video games were wide open and going strong.

Nothing else remained but the snack machines, where Eileen doled out coins for a packet of Cheese Nips and a can of cherry pop. For the next few minutes, Sasha was entirely occupied with opening her purchases, sipping and chewing. Eileen's thoughts drifted back to the man on the ground. Why did the other passengers stand there as if riveted, stare so intently? A little excitement, of course. But added to that, it struck her suddenly, was the fact that a good many of these passengers looked like they were only a step or two away from homelessness themselves. A few steps made considerable difference, she realized. She tried to imagine what it would be like to live without a roof over her head. *Must feel like having your skin barked off...*

Even inside the terminal, Eileen could feel it, the profound near-dawn chill. She needed creature comfort—warmth, bed, home, the wrap of roof and walls, family and friends, a skein of meaning to mask the outer dark. She longed for first light, seeping, filling, brimming—unstoppable. For steaming coffee and the velvet taste of cream, each least detail of morning come.

ROBERTA HIT THE PHONE BANK FIRST THING; THEIR unexpected delay gave her a good enough reason. Bob was in, but his voice was gruff. It wasn't like she was calling collect or anything, as she tried to point out; she was using the phone card she'd bought with her own money in Tucson. He wasn't mad, though, just sleepy, he explained, he'd been napping when the phone rang. He'd already called the station and learned that her bus would be coming in late. "Try calling back in an hour or so," he'd been told.

But—they *had* to talk. Roberta had lived through so many things in the past days that she thought it would take a year to tell. Yet now, when she couldn't hold in any longer and it burst out of her, the story took less than three minutes. Already they were signing off. "I love you," she said—she fell back on that. She was sick of the word *love*, her old monotone of need, but it was all she had. "I miss you," she tried.

"Same here," Bob said, sounding like he meant it, only maybe half awake . . . Was that sighing Roberta heard in the background? Or was she imagining this? She could still turn around—he'd better not think she was crawling back to him. Considering the time of night, though, maybe he was yawning, maybe that's all it was. Or maybe he was flossing his teeth, how could she tell? She couldn't be sure, and yet—that first instant, hearing his voice, how her heart had leapt! Beyond the clutch of doubt and fear . . .

With a fresh burst of energy, she hastened to the restroom. She knew what she'd do. Soon as she'd flushed, she took out her Sharpie pen; she'd already chosen a spot in plain sight of anyone sitting there. She began printing in block letters, big as the space would allow:

ROBERTA & ROBERT WRIGHT

R&R—

I AM SO HAPPY!!!

MARRIED ONE YEAR AGO

A WEEK FROM TODAY

4-17-00

Around the inscription, she drew a valentine heart for a frame, then two arrows piercing it at the same exact slant.

Finally, Roberta stepped back as far as she could manage in that cramped stall to study her work. Around it, messages gobbed the wall, some in script so tiny you had to put your eye right up to the letters to be able to read them. They were mostly what she expected: sad, angry, horny. Roberta's words were different; her letters were clear and crisp. Her message couldn't be missed.

It would stand.

Probably not for long, though. Like ants to sugar, the four-letter words soon would be swarming over it.

But, for now . . .

DEE ANNA COULD SMELL TROUBLE WAITING TO HAPPEN and hurried away from the bus, striding quickly across the waiting room, heading for the door at the opposite end.

The lot in back was where the drivers and the rest of the staff left their cars. Here, Dee Anna started pacing, up and down, always keeping the door she'd entered by—an escape hatch if she needed to run for it—in the corner of her eye. But there wasn't another soul. Everybody else was likely to be out front or standing close to the front doors. In the dark, the parked cars seemed to be sleeping, humped, motionless shapes. It was chilly out; the wind was stirring. A cup of hot cocoa would have been lovely, but Dee Anna was saving her few remaining dollars; the little purchases were the ones that did you in.

Dee Anna walked briskly, round and round, waving her arms to get her circulation going. Each time she completed a loop, she stopped and stretched: right arm, left arm, way, way up. The night sky was thronged with stars, the gnat eyes of stars . . . *A cloud of witnesses,* wasn't that the promise? But who saw it all? Who could stand it?

Her eyes trained on the heavens, Dee Anna failed to notice the sleek Trans Am shadowing her, cruising by slowly, with only its low beams on. Rage red by light of day, the car was gray now in the no light of long-past midnight. Its rear window was slatted, making it hard to see the three young men inside. On the Trans Am's second time around, a window opened on the passenger's side in front and a young man's head leaned out, a cigarette clamped to its lips. Nothing was said. Dee Anna had her back to the car at that moment, and the driver decided to make another go-round to check her over one last time. As they approached, Dee Anna sensed something at her back, there was a prickling, a tiny stitch of presentiment—*somebody out there watching*—but when she turned to look there was no one. Except for a car turning the corner, a thin streamer of smoke trailing after it.

The wind was kicking up. Dee Anna felt colder now, a bitter chill. And hunger, she couldn't argue it away. She decided to head back inside. Maybe she could load up on some packets of free saltines at the snack bar. Would it still be open at this hour? Hurrying through the waiting room on her way out here, she hadn't noticed. Most likely, the snack bar had been shut for hours, though, and if so she might have to spend some money on peanut butter crackers or a bag of pretzels from one of the machines. Or a chocolate bar—the thought was tempting—except for the fact that chocolate was only quick energy, no staying power. By now, she'd almost forgotten her worries about spotting; all she could think of was hunger, the hollow rumbling of her stomach.

". . . LIVING OFF THE REST OF US," SOMEONE CLOSE BY was holding forth. "About time one of them's getting it!" Sam failed to catch all the words but couldn't miss the enthusiasm in the man's voice.

About time . . . Of course! Why didn't Sam see what was obvious to everyone? Why did he find it all so fumbling and sad? One man sinks; the displaced water rises, and everything around the sinking one is buoyed up a little; one man's disgrace confers a kind of grace on the spectators. It was no news, and it should have come as no surprise to Sam, the way they'd started out in a loose semicircle at first, then, as things started to jell, how people

All That Road GOING

closed ranks, drew together, became, for the moment, one body. Only the man in the knit cap remained where he was, standing his distance, far enough off to signal his difference from everyone else. And he was still clutching that damn lunch box! Merely to glance at the man made Sam's heart race.

It was strange . . . as if the boundary between self and self had become porous suddenly, and Sam knew for a certainty what he'd only suspected before. The man in the knit cap was up to no good. The police had cornered the wrong person.

It now seemed transparent to Sam how evil the man's intentions were, how that lunch box, which he never let out of his hands and carried as carefully as if full of uncooked eggs or delicate glass, must be equipment for some nefarious project or other. And—Sam was willing to bet on it—that project wasn't "better living through chemistry."

Sam wanted to shout: "I don't know what you're up to, but I know it's no good." He wanted to step out and challenge the man to his face: "It's not too late to get out of it—whatever it is you're hatching . . ."

He reminded himself that he was jumping to conclusions again, he knew nothing, really. Besides . . . It defied reason why anyone hatching bomb schemes or on the run would choose to hang around in full view of the police. And yet, it seemed ever more clear to Sam, his belief all the more forceful for his arguing against it, that he had seen a police sketch in the papers yesterday, or the day before, of a bombing suspect, his features partially obscured by a hood and aviator sunglasses, with a definite resemblance . . .

Resembling wasn't the same thing as matching, of course. Unless he got closer, able to see for himself, Sam couldn't be certain.

He had to know—now.

As Sam struggled toward him, the man in the knit cap did not seem to notice at first. Then as the distance narrowed between them, he did a quick two-step, colliding with someone behind him. His arm shot up with a clattering noise. Arm and lunch box hung in the air . . .

Amazed at the blood rush, the heat, Sam found himself waving his fist in the man's face.

"Who's shoving?"—a voice from the crowd.

"Hey—go easy!"

There was an audible hush . . . one fused syllable of breath indrawn.

They all turned.

Instant

"OK," ONE OF THE COPS ADDRESSED HIMSELF TO THE MAN on the ground. "Show me your ticket! C'mon, you show me," he stooped to spring the handcuffs. "I'm clocking you . . ."

The panhandler staggered to his feet. Stood there, swaying, couldn't seem to find his footing. Sam, stopped dead in his tracks, foresaw what was coming: the man was going to take his chances and run, never mind that he couldn't properly hobble in those unlaced sneakers of his.

Worst thing he could . . .

Seven, eight beats, he stalled. Only his eyes moved, darting rapidly, mistrustfully, side to side. Then upward, spotting something above him in the air. His hand drifted, crazily, dreamily . . . pulled at his crotch . . .

That did it: Sam heard this sharp pop. A shot—one crisp bead of sound. The panhandler lifted his chin, twisting his head back over his shoulder, as if someone were calling his name from that direction, and a look of total surprise came over his face. Something metal hurled overhead—Sam ducked, so close it came.

Another sound—a crunch, a crump—and the man, who'd only just now risen, tottered, went down.

Sam recognized the lunch box, though not what tumbled out of it—the thing was oblong, black, with a rounded head. Grenade? Possibly. But it looked like nothing more than a handheld mike without a cord, a microphone unconnected to anything in the world.

A toy!—lunatic toy . . . The microphone lay where it landed, close to the lunch box. No way to tell whether it had come down wide of its mark, or what the target had been, if any—the police? Sam? The man on the ground? Sam was jolted right and left, his view cut off by a pillar; when he was able to see clear again, what looked like a thick tarp covered the lunch box and the mysterious black object. Two men—the passenger with a camera and one of the police—were already closing in on the man in the knit cap, who'd pushed his way back to the edge of the crowd but was blocked by a wall.

The police were all over the bystanders now, herding them off to a distant gate.

Sam cast a backward glance at the man on the ground. He hadn't a prayer, that was clear. The eyes he turned to the crowd were entirely white, white and indifferent now. Then his head shifted, his ear nestling close to his collarbone. And then he was still.

"¡Ay, Madrecita!" a voice cried.

AT THE INSTANT THE SHOT WAS FIRED, THE MAN STANDING next to Clem was busy popping the tab of a Coke can; the sound of the tab breaking and the hiss of escaping bubbles kept Clem from paying attention to the important sound. He missed most of the action, it was over that quick.

WHEN THE MAN WENT DOWN, SASHA WAS INSIDE THE terminal, opening a crackly bag of Cheese Nips; Eileen was guiding her hand, trying to minimize the spill. They heard nothing. Dee Anna was peeking into the alcove with the vending machines, where only the later loudspeaker announcements were able to penetrate.

PIERSON WAS TOURING THE WAITING AREA, TRYING TO outpace his headache. He'd bought some aspirin from a machine in the men's room selling combs, condoms, travel toothbrushes, and the like. He'd taken three aspirins in one swallow, but so far they weren't working, his pain gnawed on, unabated. His seatmate, the man going blind, stood, leaning one elbow on the counter of the deserted information desk. He seemed to be blessing himself with his free hand—that, or brushing off fleas—touching each shoulder, his forehead, his heart.

ROBERTA, MEANWHILE, WAS KILLING TIME. SHE COULDN'T understand what the delay was for; she couldn't concentrate; the closer she got to home, the harder it was to put up with the least separation. She paced restlessly, reading the departure and arrival schedules posted over each gate—anything to keep herself occupied. For some reason, the door to her gate had been barred by security. *Why was it taking so long?*

BY THE TIME SAM WAS ABLE TO TURN AGAIN AND CATCH A last glimpse, the panhandler had worked himself into a fetal knot. One hand peeked out—its fingers scrabbling the asphalt as though trying to take root. An officer bent solicitously over the body, leaned to the man's open mouth; standing again, he shook his head. He seemed to be signaling another officer who was speaking into a cell phone. Was the man with the cell phone the one who'd fired the shots? Had he simply switched hands? Impossible for Sam to tell, to make sense or sequence of events so jumbled, so blurred.

But talk about overkill! The man on the ground, who'd taken up so little space to begin with, seemed to be shrinking in front of Sam's eyes. Not so the blood, which seeped in long fringes, darkening as it spread. Who would have dreamed that one person, a man so insignificant, could contain so much blood?

Witnesses

VOICES MINGLED: "SU CAMINO SE ACABÓ." HIS JOURNEY has ended . . . "He was asking for it. I saw . . ." "La mierda del mundo . . ." "I can't understand a word you're saying!" A whispered: "I should of went inside."

Because the shooting was over in the blink of an eye, and because someone was popping a soda can right at that moment, it was a different story with each of them.

Someone spoke over Sam's shoulder: "Must of had a weapon. The guy was lunging—I saw him reach . . ."

Sam whirled around. "You sure you saw that?"

"Sure, I'm sure. Saw it like I'm seeing you now. Concealed weapon. Cops had every right. And that other one, that screwball, I had my eye on him. He was asking for it . . . Everyplace the same damn thing! Launch them all into outer space—the bums, the addicts, the loony tunes, the faggots, we'd all be better off . . ."

There was no weapon: Sam was sure the police had frisked the panhandler right away. It stood to reason, even if he hadn't witnessed it firsthand. But he was too exhausted to argue with a man who had all the answers. Anyone with that much energy of conviction exhausted him. People saw what they expected to see, the world blundered on.

The less said, the better; nothing Sam or anyone else could say after the fact would make a speck of difference. It happened, such things happened.

The man on the ground had been bundled off in an ambulance. Sam wasn't able to see whether the paramedics had covered his face before they shut the ambulance door. Had they ever activated the sirens? He thought not, but he couldn't recall with certainty.

The man with the lunch box had been hustled into a squad car. No question there: the police had set off with roof lights whirling, sirens blaring. Now that the sources of his irritation had been removed (as if by his personal request), Sam felt curiously empty. Idle, empty, chilled. His former bristling, it seemed, had kept him busy and warmed. But Sam had no time to stand around and wonder. A new bus was being readied for them, the bloody area was cordoned off, and Sam, along with the other passengers, was shunted over to a different boarding gate.

AT GATE 4 THE WAITING DRAGGED ON. HALF AN HOUR, AN hour, fifteen more minutes . . . The excitement had long since subsided. One of the police officers was passing out accident report forms. "Sit reps" he called them. He was especially nice, excessively, suspiciously polite. He assured them that whatever they'd left on their seats would be replaced on the same-numbered seats in the new bus. Luggage stowed in the freight compartment would be transferred. Yes, of course, they'd be looking everything over first. The bus driver followed on his heels, making sure all the passengers had writing implements and distributing a questionnaire of his own on tear-off sheets headed with the company logo.

Those passengers who'd complied with police instructions, remaining inside the terminal, had only the bus form to fill out.

There wasn't much to it, nothing really to ponder. All they were required to do was to say something about when they'd noticed the stowaway and how well they thought the driver had handled the situation. Also the name of the place they'd started from, their destinations, names of contacts and addresses. Oh, and one other thing. On the back of the sheet was a map of the inside of the bus. The seats were numbered, and each passenger had to mark his or her position with an *X*. It was rumored that the driver had turned over their ticket stubs to be photocopied for future reference. It seemed likely that every last one of the passengers was being monitored. The people who'd chosen to remain standing outside the terminal had to fill out both police and bus company forms before reboarding—a penalty paid for disregarding police instructions.

By now, they were way behind schedule, everyone delayed. A number of passengers would be missing their connecting buses, it couldn't be helped.

The smokers had lighted up again, but they puffed more slowly now and paced, going nowhere.

SAM TRIED TO STICK WITH WHAT HE COULD TESTIFY TO in a court of law, although he hoped he'd never have to. Perhaps the man with the camera had caught some of the action and they'd do a blur analysis. How many shots? Two, Sam was pretty sure of that much, but everything was over before he began to think of counting. Exactly what happened? What was the sequence? Who'd done what to whom? Proximate cause? Efficient cause? Sam couldn't say. Had it been an accident? He had no idea. It'd been a crying waste, that he knew, but there was no slot on either of the forms where such an observation might be fitted.

Only one officer had fired the shots, Sam thought. Was this an inference? An impression? He'd never actually seen a gun, it had happened too incredibly fast. One split second, a warning most likely, then another—too soon. As for the questionnaire their bus driver had given out, all Sam could say was: he'd never seen the stowaway sneak on board, and yes the driver had handled the situation competently, overall.

NOBODY CARED WHAT CLEM THOUGHT. HE COULD HAVE spit—it made him *so* mad. He was no kid. He wasn't yet nine, but he bet he could read and write better than half the deadbeats on this bus. Didn't matter that he hadn't a clue what he would say if asked, since he'd been looking elsewhere when all the excitement broke out—that wasn't the point. "Couple more years, sonny," the cop said, trying to be nice. Clem wanted to tell him where to stuff his niceness! And then the bus driver, coming around after the policeman, didn't even bother to make excuses; he simply passed Clem by in white-faced silence.

EILEEN WORRIED OVER THE QUESTIONS ON THE PAPER the driver handed her. Busy with Sasha, she'd seen and heard nothing; she'd been spared the shots and the shouting and would have to report as much. She was pleased that she remembered the driver's name at least. It was Plumlee, but his first name escaped her. She seemed to recall that the name tag he'd put up supplied only the initials: *O* and something else . . . What? Surely not O.J., but that was all that came to mind. She decided to write simply "Mr. Plumlee." And she'd add a word about his smooth driving and his patience with difficult customers. The smoothness was a bit of a stretch, but his patience was real, truly remarkable under the circumstances.

ROBERTA JOINED THE WAITING CROWD. "WHAT'S HOLDING things up?" she wanted to know. But when people tried to explain to her, she kept tuning out—the different stories were too confusing, and none of them had anything to do with anybody she knew or cared about.

But, no sweat—*give them what they want and then can we get moving?*—she filled in the slots with name, address, phone number, whatever they asked for. She *X*-ed in the square that gave her seating position on the map provided, even though she wasn't completely sure—she'd been so restless, switching around all over the place, trying to make the time pass.

The biggest empty space on the page was for her personal account of the incident. She scrawled "No comment," the only comment she could honestly make, then almost immediately scratched it out because it sounded like she knew something she wasn't telling, when in fact she didn't know a thing.

What were they waiting for now?

DEE ANNA AVOIDED THE DRIVER'S EYES AS SHE HANDED back her questionnaire. On top, she'd given her first name as Ashley but no last name and no address. As for details noticed, she'd left the slots blank, printing "sorry" in small letters at the bottom of the page.

PIERSON GAVE HIS REAL NAME BUT LEFT THE REST BLANK, except for the words "saw nothing" in caps, scrawled at a slant across the front of the page. Both Pierson and Dee Anna forgot, or omitted, to turn the page over and mark their positions on the seating chart.

Road

EILEEN'S CARDIGAN WAS ON THEIR OLD BUS; WITHOUT it, she could not get warm. It wasn't simply a question of air temperature and windchill—the air had an edge, a bite to it. The story of what had happened outside—that was the bite—was one she'd pieced together from scraps of conversation overheard here and there. It still didn't make good sense. "An accident," the officials insisted. Maybe. Did it matter now? It did. If Eileen believed one thing without the faintest tinge of doubt it was that every action, each tremor of intention, counted, made a difference. Close by you could feel that difference; farther out it was harder to perceive, but all of it added up. There was a sum, a grand total of cruelty and compassion in the world, was her conviction, and it was being tallied right now—minute by minute. It made for a temperature, a kind of human weather; as much as the ozone and greenhouse gases that newscasters fretted about, it made the planet habitable or not.

The chill, at that moment, was desolating.

Since their bus was not yet ready, Eileen and Sasha had time on their hands. It was good to be moving around, it helped restore Eileen's circulation and this generated a little warmth. Good also, in a way, that Sasha's constant tugging didn't allow Eileen's mind to dwell on any one thing for very long. Eileen made an effort to steer clear of pinball and vending machines, but what did that leave? She was at her wit's end to find other distractions. Then she spied an empty chair with a television console attached to the arm. *That might buy ten, fifteen minutes,* she thought. Half an hour, maybe, if she were lucky. She moved quickly to claim it, settled herself, then hoisted Sasha onto her lap and handed her two quarters to fit into the slot. "Me! Me! Lem-*me!*" Sasha sang out.

As Sasha surfed, with dizzying abandon, from channel to channel, Eileen allowed her eyes to close. She opened them abruptly when, only a minute or so later, she felt the child straining too far forward. What now? Sasha was trying to lick the glass. An ad for gourmet cat food was on screen: three Persian kitties were perched on a kitchen counter, singing for their suppers, their mouths glistening, their tongues like flower petals.

So—another trip to the ladies' room, to the water fountain. A walking tour of the posters on the wall, which wasn't such a fine idea since the lost and missing children required some explaining, and the pictures were placed so high that Sasha had to be lifted up to be able to see, doing Eileen's back no favor.

Finally, the loudspeakers blared. "That's us!" The straggle of waiting passengers closed ranks once more. "We're good to go." Time to move on—their bus was ready and waiting.

¿DÓNDE QUIERES IR?—PIERSON STARED AT THE SIGN, THE same one he'd started out with—*Where do you want to go?* He was no wiser now than when he'd set out. Anyway, how could it matter where? Only to be going. Motion blurred things, left nothing entirely real—that was what he wanted. Yet, for some reason, he thought of Memphis.

Had a son once, in Memphis . . . Kenny. *Ex-kid,* he reminded himself. Could be any place by now. Had a sister once. "Gone before," like they used to say . . . She'd lived all her life in Galveston, where they'd both been to high school.

Had some buddies here and there, he'd lost touch with along the way . . .

Marie had promised to take care of him. And he'd trusted her—why, he'd never know.

There must have been some announcement over the loudspeaker, the voice too fuzzed with static for him to follow. At the far corner of his vision, Pierson spotted his seatmate heading unsteadily toward him, gesturing. In no time, the man was in his face, and the first thing he said to Pierson was, "Would you please help me up the steps?"

"Steps?" Pierson echoed. The man was waiting, his arm already held out to him.

"I'll need a helping hand," he said.

Pierson reddened. *Why me?* His arm stiffened in protest. But it was useless—before he knew it, the blind man's arm was linked through his, they were latched, pressed together. *Another hook . . .*

Pierson could feel it, through their tensed arms, how the man was quaking.

The three steps, which had worried Pierson's seatmate, turned out to be four. Someone had fetched a portable step—it looked like a crate turned upside down—to ease the first giant step up. Nobody had thought of such a thing before this; it was kind of late in the game by now, and besides, a couple of passengers, not expecting or noticing the extra step, almost landed on their faces. It was more of a nuisance than anything. Trying to sweeten up the customers, Pierson figured, the company hoping to stave off any complaints or lawsuits that might be coming their way.

This booster step was no help at all to Pierson's seatmate; he'd been counting on three steps and balked, mistrustful, refusing to budge after the third. The stairs were too narrow for more than a single person at a time to manage without a squeeze, so Pierson, standing on the step below extricated his arm, handing the blind man on for the passenger at the head of the stairs to deal with; this compounded the confusion.

They resettled in silence. An awkward, almost suffocating silence. "It's been too much," Pierson started, his voice breaking in of its own accord but barely above a whisper.

His seatmate gave no sign that he had heard.

"My wife, see . . . ran out . . ."

"That old story," the blind man was quick to reply. He was busy fumbling for the lever under the armrest. Sighing, he inclined his seat as far back as it would go.

"No," said Pierson. "No, it's not what you think. I mean . . ." He couldn't say what he meant.

"Not now," his seatmate said gently, shutting his eyes. "It's much too late."

ALL THEIR THINGS SEEMED TO HAVE BEEN RESTORED AS promised, exactly as the passengers had left them in the old bus, even the seat litter seemed to be placed. It was pretty clear that everything had been examined and mapped, transferred item by item, seat by seat, the only reason it could have taken so long.

But was her cake still there? . . . Eileen, among the first to be seated, felt for the hatbox, probing with small, furtive motions of her heel so as not to draw Sasha's attention to it. All she could be sure of was that the box was still intact; beyond this, she didn't dare peek or care to speculate how battered the cake inside. Too much else to think about. She wondered instead about the other passengers, studying them as they straggled on board. What talk there was went on quietly, nobody in the mood for joking. "I don't feel safe," she heard one woman say. Some of the passengers seemed almost furtive in their movements, slinking past her. Like the man who'd resettled two rows behind her, who shuffled by with eyes cast down. His cream-colored suit, so swank when he first boarded, was rumpled and stained, and the man himself so stoop shouldered that he seemed shrunken.

The question she kept hearing, up and down the aisle, was whether the ambulance had waited until it hit traffic to turn on the sirens or whether they'd ever bothered. One thing for sure: the ambulance had left the depot in silence.

Watching them settle back in, Eileen felt it: there was something between the passengers now. Something unclean, binding.

IN AND COUNTED, IF NOT ACCOUNTED FOR . . . SAM TRIED to persuade himself that nothing had changed, but, of course, everything was different in the aftermath. What conversation there was went on more quietly. A minute ago, he thought he'd heard the rhythmic patter of prayer, a rosary perhaps. Now he was distracted by someone tapping him on the shoulder, holding out a greasy baker's box with a few doughnuts left in it. "Little late, isn't it!" Sam wanted to say. Wanted, unaccountably, to shout, "Get out of my face!"

The doughnuts were glazed pink and yellow, cheery springtime colors. Sam had all he could do to keep from reaching out and flinging the box to the floor. Instead he forced one hand into custody of the other, thumbs interlocked; his knuckles blanched. But nothing showed—not to a stranger, anyway, Sam was certain. His "no thanks" was all that surfaced, the voice squeezed out of him. The man moved on to the driver, bearing his offering plate. "No thanks" from that quarter, as well. Since taking over the wheel, the driver had made no effort to engage Sam, or anyone, in conversation. Each was left to his own silence.

Silent didn't mean resting, of course. Questions, images, swarmed his thoughts. Again, Sam saw the panhandler approach the huddle of smokers to beg for a light, swaying and billowing as he moved, so emaciated he was, so hollow cheeked when he inhaled. Clearly, he had no teeth—why wasn't this obvious before?

And why had the man stalled there, hands cupped around the match, lingering so long after the light took hold? But the answer was simple, no puzzle at all. It was only to draw the moment out, to remain standing a little while in the company of others, to be cupped himself, enclosed for a moment within the human circle.

More questions: What if he—Sam—hadn't moved so abruptly toward the man with the lunch box, so plainly determined to confront him? Had he actually waved a fist in the man's face? *Intending what?* His own actions, in retrospect, struck Sam as incomprehensible now—ludicrous—completely out of character. He'd never struck anyone in his life! Yet he'd almost. Maybe better if he had.

What if he'd reported the man earlier, right after the incident with his soup? What if—but what world ever worked like this?—Sam had chosen instead to sit back down at the table with him, and ask, "You all right? . . . Hungry as all that?" He'd have gotten a plate of soup in his face, that's what.

Sam wished at least he'd gone inside at the time of the panhandler's arrest. What was the point of standing around? His witness counted for nothing, changed nothing. He still didn't know the first thing. Over and over, the same questions: Had there been two shots or only one and an echo? One shot for warning and one meaning business? He couldn't even answer that. There'd been no special sound when the bullet, or bullets, struck meat, gristle, bone, it might have been popcorn popping had he not known.

What about that impalpable jelly, the soul?

Sam wondered about those who prayed, envied them in a way. *Happy, if delusional . . .* He'd grown up without. You couldn't miss what you'd never had, could you? In the only world he knew, entropy ruled, nothing cared; the universe was growing emptier, ever colder, there was nothing to be done. As their bus passed through the silent, unpeopled streets, all that Sam glanced upon seemed glazed, numbed into immobility, cast in a glacial light.

But he was better gazing out like this—wasn't he? Calmer, at least. Keeping his distance was the trick, taking the long perspective. It helped that there was so much he no longer really felt. Correction: *almost* no longer felt. Beverly had said some sweet things to him once, way back when. He'd come to think of those words as lies, or trifles—ear candy at best. She said, too—but that was later—"you've changed, you've lost your nerve." And this was true enough, if only partially his fault.

He needed more than anything to sleep, but doubted he'd be able, not after all the staring he'd done. Lifting off his glasses, folding the stems, Sam went through the motions of preparation for sleep, nonetheless. He eased his belt; his shoes, their backs broken for easy on and off, were quickly shed.

Yet even with eyes shut, he went on gazing, his eyelids lit from within; the light was brownish; against it, some kind of ghost ballet on endless replay. This weird synchrony: a hand slowly, dreamily, drifting . . . a crotch pulled . . . a lunch box wobbling through the air . . . all in slow motion, but none of it could be stopped . . .

WHEN DEE ANNA FINALLY LEARNED WHAT ALL THE commotion was about, she didn't connect it with her own bus. She thought it had to do with some tramp who'd happened onto some other bus. And when she heard the facts sorted out, she couldn't hold on to them in her mind. She had enough worries as it was.

Her seatmate, the witchy girl with the ratted hair, had finally cleared off. This should have brought Dee Anna a little temporary relief; if she wanted, she could stretch her legs across both seats, nobody would bother her now. Yet she remained wakeful and vigilant. In a short while, they'd be passing the transfer point for Hunters Junction. Because of their delay, she'd already missed the connecting bus. But she wouldn't have been on that bus, in any case.

It was eerie . . . Her breasts, her arms, ached, but Dee Anna couldn't turn back as her body was telling her to do. The baby was given; she'd given her baby away; there was no avoiding that fact. It was done. Over and done. At least she wasn't spotting now, and anyway she'd stashed away enough toilet paper to take care of it if she started up again.

Columbus—she must think only of that, of getting by in a city she'd never seen. Where would she go from the station? She'd have to ask where to find a bus to the YWCA, a city that big was sure to have a Y. What was so scary was not knowing anybody there. Not one person—she was casting herself loose. And—what if she'd been piling one mistake on top of another and this last decision turned out to be the biggest of them all? But what else could she do? She couldn't go back, not to anywhere she'd ever been before.

She wouldn't be going back for anything, not even the things she'd once treasured. Not for the Japanese fan or the turtle-shell mirror her mom had left to her. Not for her photo album with the genuine leather cover and the pictures she'd so carefully labeled and pasted in, with those neat little protector tabs on the four corners of each and every one. She had to let everything go. From here on out, her name was Ashley.

She wasn't scared. A little shaky from not eating for so long was all. She'd have herself a real breakfast, eggs and hash browns, bacon, and biscuits, after she'd paid for a room, when she could tell how much money she had left over.

She wasn't scared—only feeling a little emptied out. And anyway, it was good to feel a little bit scared. *The fear is my shepherd,* she told herself; it would make her more careful, she couldn't be too careful, she'd be a fool not to be scared.

My fear is my shepherd.

I shall not want.

Maybe she could cashier; she'd already done that at Allsups. Maybe she'd land a job at the same place she decided to eat breakfast—she'd have to remember to shower and change before she went out to eat, just in case. She'd have to remember to double-check that she wasn't spotting.

Dee Anna stared into the rushing darkness.

She couldn't go on forever like these past few days. Her milk would dry up tomorrow or the next day or the next . . .

A leaf zigzagged past, patted the window pane. Clung for an instant. Something small, mitten shaped, masked as a leaf.

"Not now," she breathed, "not now . . ."

CLEM COULDN'T FORGIVE HIMSELF.

He'd been looking the other way when the excitement broke, staring at a man popping open a can of Coke, thinking that was the sound he was hearing, and he'd missed the whole show. How dumb can you get! He didn't have Sasha to blame this time.

At least his skateboard was still with him—he'd checked the minute he got on board.

He missed those nifty little throwing knives he'd noticed in the grab-bag machine at the stop before this one; he'd saved money by not taking a chance at the game, but he couldn't help thinking back to them, the knives and the leather pouch for carrying them, both, they were so neat.

He missed, too, the man who'd been sitting beside him, with his crazy headset and nothing attached to it, bossing a big business that was all in his head. Clem didn't think the cops would be able to make sense of him: anybody could see he was crazy, but you had to study him a while to realize that he was way too weird, way too far out of things, to be really dangerous.

Most likely this would be Clem's last free time, his last double seat. St. Louis would be the next big stop. There, everybody would have to leave this bus and transfer to others; he dreaded the thought of again having to drag Sasha around with him wherever he went. Unless the old lady she was sitting with happened to be going on to Philadelphia, or unless he could find somebody new to take Sasha off his hands. Otherwise he'd never get quit of her. The figure of the man in the Bulls jacket came briefly to mind, along with the headachy glare of the bathroom tiles. He really couldn't make up his mind whether a person willing to pay money for Sasha was one cool dude or an asshole—a sicko—another one.

Just thinking about Sasha gave him cramps—she was such a pesky brat. Little Miss Me-Too! tagalong, always dragging him down. She'd be clinging to him all the more in a new place with people she didn't really know. Still . . . The way she'd taken to the old lady up front, the way they'd taken to each other—strangers if ever there were—was a good sign.

He had to get free of Sasha—and he would. He'd managed to put her out of mind for minutes at a time uptill now. Clem reminded himself to make the most of the time remaining. So he kicked off his sneakers. He gave the seat cushion a couple of punches to soften it. Lifting his legs to cover the place vacated for him, he drew his knees up, settled his head in the crook of his elbow, and was out like a light.

TIME TO TEND TO MY REBOARDS!

I was still pilot here, it seemed. Nobody'd offered to put in a substitute driver for the last leg of my journey, so I guessed I'd been judged fit to carry on. The bus they'd given me this time was a better, younger model—not more than a year or two old—but that was little consolation. I tried not to think back over our incident, or accident, or however you wanted to call it. The whole business struck me as avoidable and senseless. Could I have stopped it someway? If I'd looked over their tickets more carefully? Been more alert? Who knows?

I was standing in the ready room when the early-morning edition of the St. Louis paper arrived. The news was not particularly new: I paged through it slowly. The Dow was up, the Nasdaq down, interest rates holding steady; there'd been a date rape on a nearby campus; summer drought predicted in the Midwest; a U.S. policy shift toward (the name was unpronounceable); something new on breast implants; weather forecasts for the weekend: chilly—unseasonably cool; Easter fashions; picnic dos and don'ts; lawn and garden sales . . . Judging from the headlines, it might have been the dawn of any other day. What had happened here in Redmont had swelled in my mind to such an extent that I was surprised we weren't even mentioned. At the same time, I knew perfectly well that it was still too early and had been far too small a spectacle, too local, with too many blanks remaining, ever to register for much.

How did I feel? On a scale of one to ten, with one being suicide and ten winning the lottery? About a three, I guess. Running on empty, or close. The passengers weren't giving me a bit of trouble, it wasn't that. Nobody complaining too hot or too cold, no voices raised. Same cast of characters but a whole different tone to them now. Hard to put a word to it. *Sheepish*, I guess, like sheep who'd gone astray, creeping back into the fold. There'd been an eerie quiet and courtesy as they lined up to reboard. Once seated, they started dipping into their secret stashes of food and passing things around. Sharing things. Hands stretched across and up and down the aisle, and I was included in these offerings—doughnuts, chewing gum, chips, and such. How long would all this good behavior last? Through my shift, at least? I could only hope so.

I wanted to drive out of the night, step on the gas, full speed ahead over the darkest depths of it, and come up on the other side. I wanted to rub the darkness out of my eyes (as if it were only my eyes!) I wanted to be home, home at last, and never have to leave.

As we'd pulled out, I could see passengers half standing, heads twisting, trying to catch a glimpse of the place where it—what the police called an accident—had happened. But no go. They'd deliberately positioned the new bus at an angle to rule out such a view. There was some grumbling once people realized this, yet no real fuss, everybody, like I said, on best behavior. Then they settled back down, nearly all of them, and for the lucky ones sleep took over. The old lady, I noticed, was still very much awake.

Simply couldn't think, couldn't take it in. One more stop—that's all I had in mind. One more stop and I'd be able to sign out. Get to put everything behind me for a while. Right then I was ready to retire. Anybody offered me a sweet package, or even a decent one, I'd have said yes on the spot, I would. I was so beat; my hands felt like they'd been sculpted to the wheel. My back was killing me.

Redmont in my side-view mirror, then only a sprinkling of small lights trailing behind us—was I ever glad to be gone from there! Things much too jumbled to sort out and I was far too beat. It would all be explained, sooner or later. I wasn't in any hurry to hear it.

Too tired to feel. Anything. Oh, maybe a little relief that the man in the wool cap had done something actionable finally and was off my hands. I'd marked him for trouble from the first and had been waiting, in a way, ever since. I'd been right on the money there. As for the stowaway, all I drew was this huge blank. How could it be otherwise? It was way too sudden. Besides, I'd never laid eyes on him before. The incident was unfortunate, but it was pure accident—nothing deliberate, I'd done best I could, it was nobody's fault.

One thing I knew: I wouldn't be sad to see this bunch of passengers move on. I'd stopped worrying about the girl from Hunters Junction or the kids traveling on their own. Soon, they'd be somebody else's freight. I wouldn't get to see how any of their stories turned out and, for a change, I felt the better for it.

Uneven road, then washboard. Construction up ahead. The shaking kept me awake at least. Arrows, signs, sprouted like tall weeds: SLOW . . . LOOSE GRAVEL . . . MERGE LEFT . . . ROAD DOES NOT END . . .

Easy does it . . .

The new bus handled well on the graveled stretch, I will say. And before long we were out of it, fresh blacktop under us, the road lusciously smooth.

. . . The miles ticked by. Same thoughts going round—*just another day at the office, a little more eventful, more stressful than average, just another trip down the pike*—trying to convince myself that a time would come when this trip would merge with all the others, though I knew it never would. I'd be shuffling those cards, hoping to deal them out different, for a long time to come. As the weeks wore on, sure, I'd obsess over it less. Distraction is guaranteed in my line of work, I could count on some fading. For the drift is ceaseless, unresting—and senseless (as it struck me at that hour) since nothing is ever settled, nothing changed. But, east to west and west to east, I ferry them—people leaving home or going back, fleeing the home that never was, seeking the home that never would be, setting out to find or lose themselves, they'd arrive, depart, be quit of . . . Another boarding call and they'd leave, return, set forth again, dreaming out, something always beckoning up the road, around the bend, elsewhere. Always elsewhere.

EILEEN COULDN'T BEGIN TO IMAGINE WHAT SASHA thought of all these goings-on. Maybe nothing, though. The child was so easily—so blessedly, in this instance—distracted. Earlier one of the passengers had gone up and down the aisle sharing a box of pastries. Eileen declined for both of them, but Sasha's hand shot out over her lap and what could anyone do? There were doughnuts covered in peach and yellow icing, pink and baby blue and all but irresistible to a child. The one Sasha chose, joyfully smearing hands and face with all four colors, was striped like a rainbow. What with the soda pop before this, all the sugar in her system might well keep her restless and wakeful for hours yet.

During the past hours the girl's brother had made no attempt to claim her, so Eileen assumed that she and Sasha would be traveling together until they transferred in St. Louis and went on their separate ways.

The wind was up. Trees swayed; a shower of small leaves peppered the window. Sasha stretched, rose to a standing position trying to net them and, encountering only glass, started to whimper.

"I bet somebody's tired," Eileen said hopefully.

"No, ma'am!" Sasha insisted.

"I bet it's way past somebody's bedtime! I know it is, because it's way past my bedtime, and I'm all grown up!"

This wasn't working, so Eileen tried another tack: "How about playing a game?"

At the word *game*, Sasha scrunched up her eyes, smiled, and returned to sitting position.

"Well, but you've got to lean back. Or, better yet, lie back," Eileen prompted. "You can lie on my lap and you can look up at the sky—that's the way—your head on my lap and look up through the window, yes, sure you can see." It was no game; what she'd been thinking of was counting sheep, anything to bring on drowsiness. So she improvised: "What we count in this game is stars, or telephone poles, whichever's easier, and let's see how far we get."

Sasha nestled in Eileen's lap, her eyes trained on the blackness of the window.

"I'm starting now," Eileen said. "Ready? Get set . . . You count to yourself and I count to myself. All right?"

They started, trying their best to ignore the thin, horned moon nosing in at them, keeping company with the bus. There were no clouds, only a far scattering of stars, paled a little by the moonlight. Eileen stared at the kite-shaped cluster far overhead—Big Dipper, was it?—trying to count, but soon losing track; they were too hard to pick out, the separate stars, there were too many of them. Ticking off the telephone poles as they passed was easier.

She felt certain, in any case, that Sasha could not count much beyond five or six, if that many—hadn't she put up two fingers when Eileen first asked her age? Two or three? . . . Poles or stars, either way, she'd have to repeat her small sequence over and over until the monotony of it put the child to sleep.

I WAS LOST. ONE WRONG TURN CAN DO IT . . . DON'T KNOW how it happened, or when exactly I realized that we were the only ones on the road, empty miles behind us, empty miles ahead. No turnoffs. No signs to point the way. No landmarks. Ever lose your way like that?

Felt like somebody, some mighty arm, had stretched out and shunted us off to a siding, uncoupled from the main. Out of my control, though there were nobody's hands but my own on the wheel and a lone face—mine—winking on and off in the glass. It seemed I'd left the interstate behind many miles back. The road was narrow, unlined; where the shoulder began was anybody's guess. No landmarks (did I say that before?). No fence line, not one gas station or truck stop to ask directions, nothing. Could've been looping round and round the countryside, or—no way to tell—headed due west, canceling the miles we'd come. The last sign I recalled was ROAD DOES NOT END, nothing after that. Had I blinked and missed the one after, my eyes so bleared? I needed a sign. Needed to be sure of something, anything, one thing; there was nothing I was sure of. I kept thinking of the stowaway, how startled he looked when he opened that door. Up to nothing, was my guess. Harmless. He'd stumbled into a situation, something he hadn't planned on. Had no idea what. Or maybe that was just my idea, I didn't know the first thing. He had no ticket, so what could I say about him? Destination? Did he have one? A name?

It struck me then that the man really might've have had a ticket, after all . . . That case in—Sacramento was it? California anyway, someplace in California. There'd been a big hullabaloo on CNN at the time. City officials trying to clean up the park in front of a government building. The place was an eyesore, a squatters' camp of tents and cardboard huts, the benches trashed. They'd tried turning the sprinklers on the squatters and that hadn't worked, so they'd given out free bus tickets—one-way tickets out of town. Couple of other places did the same come to think of it. The tickets were for over the county line or out of state. The man might've had one of those tickets, then lost it or sold it. Traded it in for a fix, maybe.

You've got to assume people like that don't feel things like the rest of us—was what I kept telling myself. But, again, what did I know? Fat nothing is what.

I tried and failed to recall how my day (now yesterday) ever began. Had a CB radio aboard but couldn't touch it, couldn't admit another screw-up, my second in one night. My headlights semaphored into the empty dark. It was all a darkness.

Then something beckoned, glowing, in a tree. Hubcap, as I found out, snared in a web of branches. Thought to myself: *It didn't just fly, somebody must've strung it up there. Somebody must have passed this way . . . But when? Hours? Months before?* I plunged on into the night, waiting, hoping to see: my headlights slicked the road, frosting the way ahead a few yards at a time. Sheer drop, felt like, and I was tumbling—no net, no life vest, no bottom to it . . .

I kept up my speed regardless, though, like I knew what I was doing. In case anybody was watching. Scary—believe you me, I'd be lying if I said any different. You can't get lost in America, right? Wrong.

I kept giving myself advice: *Think positive, quarter moon not too bright, so you can see the stars,* that sort of thing. Helped a little, not a whole lot. If I'd known the stars, I could've hooked onto the polestar, the North Star, and steered by it, but I couldn't recognize a one, I had nothing to go by. I was blundering through deep space, drowning in it. Just the wheel in my hands, thinking of that dream I had, with the drive never ending and the steering wheel breaking off in my hands. But this was worse in a way, this was no dream.

For the first time I felt—what I don't, can't, afford to believe in the light of day—how we're all, all of us, chancing it, lost in this swirling tide, lurching along, adrift . . .

Did I see a sign?

I did, there seemed to be a mile marker up ahead. *Too good to be true,* I cautioned myself, blinking hard.

Still there. It was real, no mirage, and the thing grew larger and legible as I closed the distance.

I was back in a known country.

PIERSON'S THOUGHTS KEPT WENDING HOMEWARD, TO the home he knew he'd never go back to. Had he remembered to lock the door? Did it matter now? . . . The lakefront cottage would be standing exactly as he and Marie had left it—when?—only yesterday? Seemed like a lifetime ago . . . They'd had to leave in the middle of breakfast, beds unmade, milk pooling in their cereal bowls, everything curdled by now. He could say exactly what was in the fridge, her miso soup and bean paste, her soy milk, her wheat germ, all her vegetarian tofu crap, and that stuff in the green bottle. Whatchamacallit oil . . . *Seaweed and soy—much good it had done her!*

He missed his boots. If they'd been dining out tonight, as they did most Fridays, he'd be wearing them. When he put them on it wasn't only the stacked heels that made him feel six feet tall. They were real class—no shitkickers, those, hand tooled, made of finest light-skin lizard. How long had he had them now? Two years? They'd been a birthday present, the nicest ever. From Marie, of course. Of course—who else would it be? She'd promised to take care of him always . . .

Never grow old!

It was almost over, Pierson knew. He knew. Marie's fingers were folding in. Her lips shadow-shaped some buried word. "Pruhh . . ." You had to bend low to recognize it as a word at all.

Pierson leaned closer, lowered his head, trying to make it out: "Pruhh . . . b'h . . . ," the mask lifted away.

Her last word—was it *probably?*—could that be it? He'd never know. Only Marie's face—expressionless, a stony husk—remained sharp and clear in his mind's eye. Hard to believe a face like that had ever smiled or wept. Or that he was free.

Everything looked strange to him now. His seatmate was sleeping, no question of faking it, his head jutting over the armrest into the aisle, a painful angle. His slack mouth gaped and his breath, coming and going, gave out a faint fizzing sound. Unwatched, Pierson was free to laugh or curse or cry. Raw sounds escaped him—famished swallows of air. He'd crossed some boundary this time, unmarked but unmistakable, some border of the mind. He'd become strange to himself.

He'd put himself on this bus and kept on going to be free of Marie, her dying on him, her broken promise, the promise he'd never made. But the more he ran, the farther away he got, the more she filled every crevice of his mind. She'd stopped calling his name, and it was only now he listened for it. No one was calling him now.

Pierson sat hunched forward, head bowed, hands clapped to his face, trying to contain sounds he could not recognize as his own. He tried to cough: something thick, clogging, he had to clear it from his throat. It would not come. What came were tears, seeping through the slats of his fingers, soiling his collar. Wetting himself! As sorry a sight as if he'd wet himself. *As sorry* . . . Digging deep in his pocket for his hanky, Pierson touched metal, a coin, then—what was it?—a ring, the ring he'd given her after their first year together, its diamond no bigger than a crumb. Yet she'd treasured it, soaping it off her finger only at the last minute, and handing it to him for safekeeping, right before they left for the hospital. He'd forgotten all about it.

What else had he forgotten?

She'd hooked him, no question . . .

Sorry . . . That was the suck word, the clump, the clog, the gobbet that stuck in his craw. He was lost, terribly lost. As if Marie had been breathing him, dreaming him, and he was dreamt no longer.

He was just going along, speeding along, nothing impeding now. No choke chain, no anchor . . .

He was perfectly free.

EILEEN SPOTTED THE JET PASSING OVERHEAD, DIPPING dangerously close to the ground, barely skimming the power lines. In trouble, had to be. It couldn't be coming in for a normal landing—there was no sign of any airport nearby. Its booming wake made even the new bus sound rickety, ancient; the floorboards juddered, windows ticked; bones, teeth, jangled; screws rattled in their sockets.

Then it was past.

Even after the booming subsided, Sasha kept lifting her head to let Eileen know that she wasn't asleep yet. Eileen had reached seventy-two before the plane interrupted her but had to break off and start the count all over again from scratch because—Sasha was getting herself quite worked up over this—the child didn't know whether they were supposed to be counting stars or poles, which was it?

They should have been counting sheep, but Eileen had decided against them from the outset because there were no sheep to be seen; they would have to be sheep in the mind only, and that would have been too hard to explain. So she had to decide, to choose. Should it be stars or telephone poles when they started over? Eileen decided on stars, because they were harder to pick out than poles and she hoped they'd blur and bring on slumber more quickly. She'd do the counting for both of them this time. She started counting aloud in a slow monotone.

Soon, her chanting accomplished what she'd hoped for. Snug up against Eileen's ribs, Sasha slept at last. The child seemed folded into sleep, her features simplified, mere creases for mouth and eyes. *You'll not remember me.* Eileen smoothed the girl's tousled hair. *Can't help wishing, though.* Her hand moved lightly, rousing only the faintest breath-stir of passage.

It was a wonder . . . a stranger's child, and strange besides, so blindly trusting . . .

Star of wonder . . .

Right then, out of nowhere, hours too late, the verse she'd been struggling to recall came to her:

> Star of wonder
> Star of light
> First star I see tonight
> Wish I may, wish I might
> Have the wish I wish tonight

Eileen picked one star, brighter and steadier than all the rest, and wished the past two hours undone. She knew the minute she'd shaped the thought this wasn't how it worked; you could only wish forward, not backward—she'd wasted her wish. Besides, this was far from the first star she'd seen tonight, but many stars, whole flocks of stars, later. She wondered what the child might have wished for.

What time was it? She didn't dare switch on the reading light and check her watch. The child slept on, let her be. Weary to the bone, yet wakeful, Eileen could only gaze out. The window was a dark mirror with flickering lights, the intermittent bright cloud of a face. She leaned closer. The face was her own but so bleached and harrowed that her heart plummeted.

FORGET HOURS AND MINUTES—IT'S LATE, PLENTY LATE. Peering through the face, as through a veil, its gauzy surface thins; Eileen sees car lots and salvage yards sweep past. Power lines unspool . . . Billboards proclaim and vanish. Stars, drifting, slip from containment beyond the borders of the frame. The world is slipping away . . . She touches one hand to the glass.

Then turns.

Inside the bus, around her, a deep, lightless well. She listens. The sound is muffled but coming through—close, but not next to her, two, maybe three rows back. No one is speaking. Something else.

Behind her, she hears a man weeping in darkness . . .

About the Author

A. G. Mojtabai is the author of eight previous books, including the novels *Mundome, A Stopping Place, Autumn,* and *Ordinary Time;* the story collection *Soon: Tales from Hospice;* and the nonfiction study *Blessèd Assurance: At Home with the Bomb in Amarillo, Texas.* Among her awards are the Lillian Smith Book Award for the best book about the American South and the Award in Literature from the American Academy of Arts and Letters. She has taught at Harvard University, New York University, and the University of Tulsa and now lives in Texas.

Also by A. G. Mojtabai

Mundome

The 400 Eels of Sigmund Freud

A Stopping Place

Autumn

Blessèd Assurance: At Home with the Bomb in Amarillo, Texas

Ordinary Time

Called Out

Soon: Tales from Hospice